MALICE

THE AEGIS OF MERLIN
BOOK ELEVEN

JAMES E WISHER

SAND HILL PUBLISHING

Edited by: Janie Linn Dullard

Cover art by: Paganus

ISBN: 978-1-68520-043-5

60220231.1

1

Malice Kincade didn't know exactly what to make of her situation. She was surrounded by endless darkness. Her feet weren't resting on anything solid. In fact, as far as she could tell, she didn't even have feet. When she tried to turn her head to look around, it didn't feel like she even had a head, much less a neck or anything connected to it. In her many years, she had never experienced anything like this. Even when she freed her spirit from her body, she could feel the old, worn-out husk waiting to welcome her back to its painful embrace.

In the absolute darkness, time meant nothing. For all she knew, she might have been hanging around this place for days or decades. The last memory she had before arriving here was a wall of white flame roaring toward her, an instant of pain as it consumed her flesh, then nothing.

If she'd had a face, she would've snarled. Conryu Koda had controlled the white fire. That boy had caused her nothing but trouble since she first had the ill luck to set her gaze upon him. Despite all the potential that his genes carried, she would've been better off killing him out of hand. But no, she'd been so damn confident, so proud, so certain that the Kincades' power would eventually allow her to bend him to her will that she'd schemed and plotted instead of acting.

And now look what had become of her. She was dead. The power of those white flames allowed no other explanation. But everything Malice knew about the afterlife indicated that she should have become one with Hell's essence as soon as her soul arrived. She'd made no prior arrangement with the Reaper after all.

Becoming one with Hell's essence while retaining her awareness was about the worst fate she could imagine.

"Then you need to expand your imagination, mortal." A deep voice, heavy with power, spoke from all around her. "I had expected more from the great Malice Kincade."

The way the voice said "great" held so much derision it was almost a physical thing. Malice's pride bristled at the insult.

"Who are you?"

Endless jungle replaced endless darkness in the blink of her eye.

Eye? She had eyes? Her hands went to her face before she had time to be surprised to have either. Everything felt as it should, neither improved nor degraded.

Malice lurched as her body rose into the air. She was standing on a hand bigger than her favorite limo that appeared to be made of vines and rotted wood. The hand connected to an arm longer than Kincade Manor. At the end of it was a body the size of a skyscraper, made of the same jungle detritus.

When she reached a place a few feet from the giant's face, it glared at her with glowing red eyes twice as big around as she was tall. Malice swallowed and tried not to let her nerves show. She'd dealt with many demons over the years, but nothing on the scale of this creature.

"Who am I?" Breath that stank of rot washed over her. "I am Baphomet, Lord of the Corrupt Earth. And you are in my hell."

"Not the Reaper's?" she asked before thinking better of it.

"You were slain in my temple; snatching your soul and bringing it here was a simple matter. Perhaps you would prefer to be in Null's hell? Given your relationship to his Chosen, I'd think you'd be pleased with your final destination."

A demon lord. One of the most powerful beings in existence. For all her years of experience, nothing could've prepared Malice for this. Still, if Baphomet had snatched her soul out of the Reaper's grasp and deigned to speak to her face-to-face, it had to mean he wanted something. And if he wanted something, Malice had room to negotiate.

Baphomet's laughter knocked Malice on her backside. "You think you can negotiate with me? Pathetic wretch of a mortal, your soul is mine, to shape, torment, or destroy as I see fit. The only reason you retain your will is because I allow it. The task I require will be easier if you have your full range of faculties. Easier, mind you, but don't think for a moment that I won't punish you should you make my life difficult."

Malice worked her way back to her feet. "I'm already dead. What sort of punishment could you give me?"

"Perhaps you'd like a demonstration."

Pain unlike anything she'd experienced raced through Malice. Spasms wracked her body as her essence was shredded an inch at a time. It made the white flames' embrace feel like a sunburn.

And then the pain vanished and she was once more standing on Baphomet's outstretched hand. "I can make the pain eternal. I can make it worse. Defy me, wretch, and I will show you torments beyond imagining. Pain so vast it would drive you mad. Only I won't grant you that mercy. You will be awake and aware for all time, with no respite from your agony."

"I understand. Your point was well made." Malice took a small measure of pride at how calm she sounded. "How may I be of service?"

"Much better. That's the sort of attitude I like to see in my slaves."

Malice didn't even take offense at the description. Doing so would've been like an ant taking offense at the human that flicked it off the picnic table.

"Very soon, my Chosen on your world will complete a summoning ritual. You will pass through it and serve as his guide. A new temple must be built and consecrated. An army of thralls raised. And at last the world conquered. My Chosen is strong, but not wise or worldly. That's where you come in. Guide him well and you shall help him rule your world. Guide him poorly and you know what awaits you here."

Malice nodded. "Will I still have my magic when I return?"

"In a manner of speaking. All your magic will come from my hell. Only darkness and corrupt earth will answer you now. The other elements will be closed to you and should you attempt to use them, they will punish you for it." The demon lord chuckled again. "You are a clever woman, for a human. I have great confidence that you will master your new abilities quickly and make the most of them. Highly motivated slaves tend to be fast learners. In fact, you can practice here until the ritual is ready."

Baphomet turned his hand slowly over and soon Malice found herself falling far too quickly toward the distant ground. While she doubted the impact would destroy her, she felt certain that it would hurt like hell.

2

Despite the late hour, the forest teemed with activity. Owls hooted, insects buzzed, and every once in a while, the faint scream of something dying filled the air. And animals weren't the only busy ones; Miguel, the Chosen of Baphomet, also labored. He had been working to create a magic circle powerful enough to connect this world to his master's hell. It had to be done in a specific way, or so his master had indicated during his occasional visits to Miguel's dreams. The why remained a little vague, but he knew better than to question his master.

He was also forced to work at night when the druids slept lest the wizards among them realize what he planned.

The magic was vastly more complex than anything he had tried before. That complexity had led him to numerous failures, but now he'd nearly completed the circle. With any luck and another hour of work he could finally summon the demon that would guide him in furthering his master's goal.

Miguel sighed and took a deep lungful of the slightly damp air, spicy with the scent of cedar and spruce. He liked it here, so different than the little island where he grew up, with its harsh heat, salty wind, and grinding poverty. Sometimes, in the very deepest, most secret part of his mind, he wondered if it wouldn't be better to just forget about Baphomet and resign himself to a quiet life with the druids.

He snarled the thought away. Miguel would never go back to being such a weakling. Besides, his soul belonged to the demon lord and when he died, a horrible fate would await him should he fail.

Not that Miguel had done much besides fail since becoming a hellpriest.

He clenched his fists and banished all thoughts of weakness. They belonged to the old him. That simple fisherman was as dead as his parents. He would conquer this world for Baphomet and rule it as a king.

Focusing himself, he made the final ethereal connections. The summoning circle filled the clearing the druids called home. It glowed with an ugly red light, the intricate runes seeming to writhe around like living things. Now he had only to activate it.

And to do that he needed sacrifices.

But first he concentrated and the black robes that marked him as a hellpriest appeared around him. He'd hidden his true nature for far too long.

Miguel raised his hands and the ether sped his will into the plants surrounding the clearing. Vines rushed out from every direction, smashing into the crude huts that served as the druids' homes. Men and women were yanked out, wrapped head to toe by the black vines.

Their mouths were covered to keep them from asking questions Miguel didn't want to answer. Bad enough that he had to answer those questions in his own mind.

When all the druids had been dragged into place around the circle, Miguel shifted the flow of ether into the circle. Life force flowed down the vines, reducing the sacrifices to lifeless husks. Moment by moment the circle glowed brighter.

A black globe appeared in the center of the circle and slowly expanded until it had grown nearly as tall as Miguel. Then it popped like a balloon, leaving behind an old, hunched-over woman in a black robe. She had more wrinkles than anyone Miguel had ever seen and he'd seen eighty-year-old men who'd spent their entire lives trying to wrest a living from the ocean.

The old woman looked around, the wrinkles shifting as her scowl deepened. Finally her crimson gaze settled on Miguel. She looked neither impressed nor subservient. Miguel hadn't known exactly what to expect when his new demon guide arrived, but an elderly human certainly wasn't it.

"So, you're the Chosen of Baphomet." Contempt dripped from her every word. "I understand why he thought you needed a guide. I doubt I've ever seen anyone so unsuited to his current role. What's your name, boy?"

That was one insult too many. "Miguel, but you may call me Master."

"Make me."

He stared for a second, uncertain he'd heard correctly. "What?"

"I said, make me. Use your magic to compel me to obey. Surely that's not too much of a task for the great and powerful Chosen of Baphomet."

"I summoned you." Miguel hated how weak and trembly his voice sounded. "That should be enough to make you obey."

The old woman shook her head. "Why in the world did Baphomet pick an ignorant whelp like you for his Chosen? There had to be better options. We'll just have to make do. Where are we, boy?"

"Washington state." Exasperated by the situation, Miguel said, "At least you could introduce yourself."

"You may call me Malice. Washington is better than I'd feared. Our West Coast campus is in California, not that far south, especially for someone that can use magic. Well, someone that can use it properly. That leaves both of us out. Who'd have thought there'd be so many limitations after being reborn as an immortal demon?"

She seemed to be talking more to herself than Miguel, but he asked, "If you're a demon, why do you look like that?"

"I didn't start out as a demon, boy, I was reborn as one in Baphomet's hell. This is what I looked like when I was human. Do you at least know how to make thralls?"

"Yes, though it's much harder without the Black Eternals."

"That's something at least. Animate the corpses and I'll see about turning them into something useful."

Why was the demon giving orders to her summoner? Probably because the summoner lacked the strength to do anything about it. He swallowed a sigh and sent Baphomet's power into the bodies. Black vines, tiny as threads, quickly spread through them. They had barely started to rise when the vines he'd summoned to collect his sacrifices impaled them and ripped them apart.

Miguel was about to ask what she was doing when the amalgam of flesh and wood began to shape itself into something else. His jaw dropped as wings and a wide, flat body appeared along with a skinny pair of legs.

"It's a bird. But it must be too heavy to fly."

"You really are a fool," Malice said. "So much power and no skill to wield it. What a shame. I'd need a decade to properly educate you, but our master isn't the patient sort, so this task will go more smoothly if you just do as I say. Once we rule the world, I can give you proper lessons."

Since he had no real rebuttal to make, Miguel decided it would be less embarrassing for him to stay silent.

A moment later he nearly landed on his ass as a massive vine carried him onto the bird's back. Malice landed beside him a moment later.

The creature beat its wings and they were soon airborne and heading south. He didn't know how far they could get before sunrise, but doubted it would be a good idea to go flying around on this thing when people might see them.

For now, much as Malice suggested, he was content to let her take the lead. It seemed she had a plan at least. That was more than he could say despite having weeks to think of one.

Some Chosen he was turning out to be.

3

Conryu lay in bed and stared at the white ceiling, a big, dopey grin on his face. The source of his grin shifted in her sleep, snuggling deeper under the covers. Maria had helped him thoroughly test the effectiveness of the dragon bone ring the forge master had made for him. The tiny ring rested comfortably on his right little toe and absorbed the corruption he constantly shed since his brief time serving as the Reaper's replacement. As long as he wore it, Maria felt no pain when she touched him.

All aspects of the test had been glorious, totally worth the wait. In fact, last night had been so glorious that as soon as Maria woke up, he hoped to perform the test again just to make sure he hadn't missed anything.

He yawned and turned his head a fraction. On the nightstand beside the bed, a digital clock flashed nine o'clock. Somehow, he'd thought it was later. They didn't exactly get to sleep early last night. From the closed drawer he sensed Prime's annoyance at being locked up. His ill-mannered familiar never appreciated having to keep out of sight, but last night Conryu had needed at least the illusion of privacy.

If this was going to be a regular thing, and he dearly hoped it would be, they might have to get their own place. Shacking up in a hotel room was okay for a night here and there, but it was going to get expensive after a while. They could've gone to his cabin on the floating island, but there was no cell service up there and Maria didn't want to be out of contact.

Like the most beautiful gopher ever, her head popped out from under the covers. "Hey."

"Hey yourself." Conryu kissed the top of her head, getting just a hint of citrus from her favorite shampoo. "How are you feeling?"

"Slightly sore, but mostly awesome." She wiggled closer and rested her head on his chest. "I was starting to think last night was never going to happen."

"You and me both. I'm going to have to buy the forge master a bottle of whatever demons drink in the Reaper's hell."

"Buy him two, I'll chip in."

"Speaking of seconds…" He leaned in for a kiss.

Their lips were just inches apart when Maria's cellphone rang. She pulled away and reached for it.

He groaned. "Let it go to voicemail."

"Can't, that's Dad's ringtone. Might be an emergency."

She reached for the phone and he stared at the pale curve of her back. Hopefully it was just some routine matter and they could get back to the fun.

Since when do you have that sort of luck?

He shot a very pointed and unkind thought at his familiar. Prime was right, of course. A hellpriest had probably gone on a rampage somewhere. Or a demon portal opened in downtown Central. Or the Reaper alone knew what else.

"Hey, Dad. What's up?" She listened for a moment. "How late is he? Okay, I'm on my way. Yes, I'll bring him with me."

Conryu swallowed a sigh. That hadn't sounded good and if Mr. Kane wanted Maria to bring him along, it had to be serious. So much for seconds.

"What was that about?"

"Jonny missed his last check-in and his handlers have lost track of him. He's been fighting his way up the rankings and last night he was supposed to be meeting the person behind the underground fighting ring. Dad sounded worried."

"What about you? I know you'd pretty much given up on him after he sold me out."

"Yeah, well, I'm still pissed at him, but that's not the same thing as wanting him dead. Jerk though he might be, Jonny's done his best to help out however we asked since he was assigned to the team. I'd feel bad if anything serious happened to him."

"What if something minor happened to him?"

Maria grinned, kissed him on the cheek, and rolled out of bed. "That's what healing magic is for. I'm getting a shower."

"Want some company?"

"No time. I'll take a rain check though."

Conryu sighed as the bathroom door closed behind her. Someday he was going to do something enjoyable without getting interrupted. Tossing his covers aside, he collected his clothes but didn't put them on. Instead he let Prime out of the drawer and summoned the library door.

"Ugh," Prime said. "Couldn't you have at least spared me the sight of your nakedness?"

"You've seen me naked plenty of times. What's the big deal?"

"The previous times you were in a less excited state."

Conryu looked down. "Oh, right. Don't worry, that won't last long now. Come on, we're going back to the island so I can clean up. I want to be ready when Maria's done."

The shift from their hotel room to the floating island took only an instant. He emerged in front of a pool with a waterfall splashing down. It made a perfect natural shower not to mention looking gorgeous. Pity he didn't have time to enjoy it.

Ten minutes later he was washed, had dried himself off with a combination of wind and fire magic, and gotten dressed.

"Why go to any trouble for that traitor?" Prime asked as they entered the library.

"I never really thought of him as a traitor. He's a soldier and he was following orders. The situation sucked, but Jonny and I have been friends pretty much our whole lives. You can't let one little disagreement get in the way of that."

"He led you into a trap that might well have ended with your death. That's a good deal worse than a little disagreement."

Conryu stepped out into the hotel room. The shower was still running, just as he knew it would be.

"Do you really think I'm weak enough that a handful of soldiers, magic-blocking crystals or not, would've been able to take me, especially with Kai keeping watch?"

"Perhaps not, but it's the principle of the thing."

"Your offended principles are duly noted. Melina."

Maria's ninja bodyguard appeared and took a knee, followed a moment later by Kai. "I'm at your service, Chosen."

"I need you to swap places with whoever's on duty keeping an eye on Maria's dad and send her here. I want to know what's going on with Jonny."

"As you command." Melina vanished into the borderland.

"Do you think there's going to be trouble?" Kai asked.

"How long have we been together, Kai?"

"A little over four years, Chosen."

"And in that time has there ever not been trouble?"

The black mask covering her face twitched. Someone that knew her less well wouldn't have noticed, but Conryu recognized that as a sign that she was smiling.

"No, I suppose there hasn't."

"Exactly. Until I know what's going on, I'm going to assume the worst: that we're about to run into some horrible monster in need of killing. If it turns out I'm wrong, so much the better."

A ninja appeared and took a knee. "You summoned me, Chosen?"

"Indeed I did. I'm not sure if we've met, but if we have, I fear I've forgotten your name. I apologize for that. Please introduce yourself and tell me what Mr. Kane has been saying with regard to Jonny's disappearance."

"My name is Min, Chosen. Chief Kane had a very tense conversation with someone named Ronan this morning. I only heard one side, but from what I gathered, this fellow was supposed to handle communication between the backup team and Jonny. The most recent check-in window passed with no word from him. Mr. Kane encouraged him and the rest of the team to find out what was going on in no uncertain terms. He then slammed the phone down."

Conryu chewed his lip. "Not a lot to go on. Well, I'll get more details from the chief. Thanks, Min."

She lowered her gaze to the floor. "I wish I could have offered more details, Chosen. And please, never feel like you need to apologize to me. It is a great honor to speak to you."

Conryu grinned. That was one thing you could always count on the ninjas for—they never complained. "If I mess up, I apologize for it. It's simple politeness. You can swap back with Melina. And keep up the good work."

She vanished and Kai said, "You spoil them, Chosen. My sisters will get soft."

"I doubt Kanna will allow that." He cocked his head. "Shower's off. Maria will be ready in a few more minutes."

"As will I." Kai bowed and vanished.

Conryu was pretty sure Kai was always ready, but he knew what she meant.

A few minutes turned out to be ten, but when Maria emerged from the bathroom she was dressed in a gray pantsuit and her hair was tied back in a neat ponytail.

"Where did you hide that outfit? You were wearing the robe your mother made for you last night."

14

"In my pocket. One of the Department wizards taught me a spell that lets you change the size of an object of limited mass. One of my outfits is about the max I can handle. It is handy though. Shall we head for the Department?"

"Sure." Conryu opened the library door and they stepped in. "Prime, do you know how to shrink things like that?"

"No, Master. That's a light magic based spell, I believe, and outside my area of expertise. I'm certain you could manage it with little more than force of will."

Conryu nodded. He didn't really use spells as such anymore, instead he commanded the ether to do what he wanted and it did. Handy for him, but he couldn't teach anyone else to do it. With a thought he shifted them to the Department and opened the door in front of Mr. Kane's office.

"I'll never get used to how convenient that is," Maria said as she reached out to knock on the door.

"How many times have I told you to use the front door?" They turned at the sound of the disagreeable voice to find Mr. Kane's secretary, Amy, glaring at them. Middle-aged and plain, she generally had the temperament of a pit bull with arthritis.

"Sorry, Amy," Maria said. "Dad called and it sounded like a bit of an emergency."

"Just don't make a habit of it." Amy's sour expression smoothed and she pressed the intercom. "Your daughter and Mr. Koda are here, sir."

"Send them right in."

Maria pushed the door open and Conryu followed her into her father's office. For a Department head, it wasn't all that plush. A sprawling oak desk dominated the room, and behind it, a couple of overloaded bookcases strained under the weight of many volumes. The only truly remarkable thing about the office was the view. You could see most of Central from here.

Mr. Kane stood and motioned them into the empty chairs in

front of him. "Thanks for getting here so quickly. Conryu, I know you're not on the best terms with us, but I appreciate you coming in."

Conryu swallowed a snarky reply and sat beside Maria. "So what's the deal?"

"I'd better give you a little background first. Word of bodies that had been beaten to death reached us about a month ago. Normally that isn't something the Department would be worried about, but every body had a lingering aura of magic—different elements, but always tinged with dark."

Conryu's eyes narrowed. That sounded like how the new demon lords' magic worked.

"It was strange enough that we agreed to join the Central police's investigation. Not long after, word began to spread about an underground fight club that specialized in death matches. Given the state of the bodies, everyone involved agreed that this was a likely avenue to pursue. We took the lead and Mr. Salazar, being our best hand-to-hand combatant, went undercover to try and find the people behind the fights."

"You sent Jonny in knowing this might be connected to the new demon lords?" Conryu asked, a cool edge to his tone.

"He was the best choice and we took every precaution." Mr. Kane didn't sound the least bit contrite. That surprised Conryu less than he would've liked. "Anyway, the investigation was proceeding well. Jonny quickly found a place where they held... I suppose you'd call them preliminary matches, and started winning. There was no magic involved yet, but he had drawn the eye of one of the big shots."

"Who?" Conryu asked. "Sounds like someone I might want to talk to."

"We don't know his actual name, but he goes by Big Bob."

"You're kidding," Maria said.

"Don't I wish. Big Bob invited Jonny to the main event two days ago. The fight was supposed to be in the basement of a gym

16

called Fists of Steel. He went in and never came out. We've had no contact since. The rest of the team searched the area and found nothing. An interview with the gym owners—this was done under magical observation so we're certain they didn't lie—made it clear that they know nothing about the fights. And that's where we are."

"Just to confirm," Conryu said. "What you're asking is for me to look into this, find Jonny, and deal with whoever's behind it all, right?"

"Exactly." Mr. Kane ran a hand over his bald head. "I shouldn't be saying this, but there are things you can do that we, constrained as we are by the law, can't. I would've brought you in at the start, but we didn't really know enough then and you were busy with the vampire thing in the Dragon Empire."

"Okay," Conryu said. When Mr. Kane's face lit up in a huge smile, Conryu continued, "I'll need you to pull your people back. I don't want them underfoot while I'm working."

"That's a problem. We're still trying to build a case against the operators of the underground fight ring. If you find anything relevant to the case, we'll need to take it into custody."

"If there's a hellpriest involved, and from what you said about the magic, it's almost certain there is, your people will be in danger. I can't do what I need to if I'm worried about them. If they show up or get in the middle of things, that's on them."

"Fair enough." Mr. Kane stood and held out his hand. "Thank you again for helping us out with this."

Conryu shook with him. He was fairly sure the Department was just using him to clean up their mess, but if they'd uncovered a hellpriest, everything else went out the window.

Besides, he couldn't just let Jonny get himself killed.

———

Orin Kane rubbed his tired eyes. Having Conryu on the job should've taken the weight off his shoulders, yet he couldn't deny that he still felt like he was on the edge of a disaster. Of course, since the business with the new demon lords began, he felt like that every day. He didn't sleep well anymore. Instead, he lay awake staring at the ceiling and imagining all the potentially horrible things that might happen.

His stomach gurgled and acid burned the back of his throat. He was also fairly sure he was developing an ulcer. Given his own state, he wondered how Conryu remained so calm.

He was debating an early lunch when the phone rang. By everything holy and good, please let it not be another problem.

"This is Kane."

"Director Kane, my name is Anders, out of the Seattle office. We've had a bit of an incident here and when I did a background check, your name popped up."

"The thing with the druids or whatever they call themselves? I thought that was cleared up and marked as a false alarm."

"It was, but last night a civilian wizard that happened to be camping with her family in Cascade National Park sensed a powerful burst of dark magic. She called it in this morning as soon as she got back into cellphone range. Given the location, we're confident it came from the camp."

Orin swallowed a long string of curses. This couldn't be happening. Not now. "Can you dispatch the same team as last time? They might notice if anything is different."

"Yes, sir. That's what I assumed you'd want. The agents are already on their way. As soon as I have a report for you, I'll be in touch."

"Thanks, Anders," Orin said, not meaning it for a moment. "Don't forget to remind them that the utmost care must be taken. At the first sign of danger, they're to retreat. No unnecessary risks."

"Understood, sir. Those are our standing orders in any case."

Orin hung up, the acid in his stomach churning even worse than before. Why did all the problems have to appear at the same time?

And more importantly, why, in the Goddess's name, had he wanted this job so bad?

4

onny Salazar had done some crazy shit over the last few years. He'd gotten mixed up in fights with demons, undead, and crazy wizards. By some miracle he'd come out of all of those in one piece. Given that, he hadn't thought twice about volunteering for an undercover mission. He often felt like dead weight at the Department, so this had seemed like a good way to contribute something to the team.

Looking back on it, that might not have been the best decision.

He shifted on the uncomfortable cot he'd been assigned and peered around the dimly lit dormitory he currently shared with thirty-one other fighters. Thirty-one smelly, snoring fighters. He shuddered and tried to take shallow breaths. Even the barracks back in Miami hadn't smelled this bad. Of course, they had showers there. He'd seen nothing here beyond a row of stalls, each of which housed a toilet that hadn't been cleaned this decade.

He tapped his pocket and frowned. Right, no cellphone. Whoever was in charge of this fight had ordered everyone to turn over any electronics before they were ushered through some sort of magical portal. It reminded Jonny of the ones Conryu opened, only instead of sending him to one of the magical realms, it dropped him here.

Having visited Hell on several occasions, he could say with great confidence that this dump wasn't an improvement.

A nearly blinding light filled the room, forcing him to blink a few times as he sat up on the cot. All around him, fighters were groaning, cursing, muttering, and generally letting their displeasure be known. The dorm's door opened and a lean, scarred man stepped in. He wore a tank top that showed his many muscles to good effect. Jonny didn't know what sort of life he'd lived, but there was hardly an inch of visible skin unmarked by a scar. Even his face had scars across the forehead and both cheeks.

"Alright, you lot!" the scarred man said. "On your feet. You're about to meet the bosses, then we'll feed you, and tomorrow morning the first round will begin."

Jonny swung his feet over the side of his cot and slid them into his boots before tying them up tight. Meeting the bosses was exactly what Jonny was supposed to be doing. Unfortunately, he had no way of contacting Ronan and letting the man know what was going on. The fact that he had no idea where he was didn't help matters in the least.

Hopping to his feet, Jonny did a few squats and stretches to work the kinks out before striding over to the scarred man like he hadn't a care in the world. One of the many things he'd learned on this assignment was that showing any fear or doubt marked you as weak and brought the sort of attention he didn't want.

"So what's for breakfast?" he asked.

"Whatever's put in front of you. Do I look like the cook?" The scarred man glowered at Jonny, and what a glower it was. The scars all seemed to deepen as his face scrunched up. If he looked into a mirror like that, it was apt to shatter.

Jonny shrugged. "You look like you're in charge. I assumed that meant you knew what was on the menu."

"Well, I don't, so shut up and get in line."

Since he was the first one to reach the area near the door, Jonny just stood and waited. It took about five minutes for the other fighters to line up behind him. As soon as they did, the scarred man led them out of the dorm and down a stone tunnel. They passed a closed door behind which came the scent of roasting meat, making Jonny's mouth water. They hadn't eaten anything since they arrived here, wherever here was, and his stomach had begun to wonder if his throat had been cut.

Another twenty yards brought them to a stone ramp that rose into the sand-covered floor of an arena. There were hundreds of seats, all empty at the moment. Three men dressed in fine suits stood waiting for them in the center of the arena. The one on the left looked about a hundred pounds overweight, and sweat ran off the rolls of fat around his neck before staining the front of his white silk shirt. Beside him was another fellow as skinny as the first man was fat. He looked like a cadaver someone had dressed in a gray suit.

Jonny's gaze shifted to the third man. He stood a pace behind the other two and wore all black, even his tie. He had a bronze, Mediterranean complexion and the hard expression of a man that had seen combat. He reminded Jonny of some of the older soldiers he'd met, only darker—that didn't mean his skin tone. Just looking at him sent a shiver up Jonny's spine.

"All right, pay attention, you louts!" the scarred man said. "These three gentlemen are the operators of this establishment. We have Mr. Bund on the left, Mr. Cadus on the right, and Mr. Asterion at the rear."

The scarred man offered a polite bow.

The corpse-looking man, Cadus, took another step to the fore. "Gentlemen, first let me congratulate you on reaching this point. You are the winners of all the selection tournaments in Central. Each of you has proven himself a capable and deadly fighter. The tournament draw has been prepared and this time tomorrow the audience will arrive. It's a who's who of the rich and decadent. I trust you won't disappoint them."

"What does the winner get?" someone behind Jonny demanded.

"I was about to go over the rules, but I suppose we can skip to the most important part. The winner will get power beyond anything he's ever imagined. Power that will make you unstoppable, like a god among men."

"I came here for money!" someone else shouted.

Asterion snapped his fingers and a magic circle appeared on the floor. Out of it rose a treasure chest that would've been right at home in a pirate movie, complete with heaps of gold and gems.

"I trust that will be a satisfactory first prize," Cadus said.

No one said anything. They were probably struck dumb at the sight of so much gold, just like Jonny.

"Splendid," Cadus continued. "Now the rules. They're simple: each pair will enter the arena, where wizards in our employ will enchant their bodies with elemental energy. The power will, temporarily, be yours to use as you see fit. You will fight until one of you is dead. The winner will have all his injuries healed and move on to the next round. The tournament will continue until only one of you survives. That person gets the treasure and the power I mentioned earlier. Simple. Are there any questions?"

A few seconds passed in silence. "Very good. Loong, get them some breakfast then meet us in the office."

"Yes, Mr. Cadus," the scarred man, Loong, said. Turning to the fighters, Loong continued. "All right, chow time. Follow me."

Loong led them back to the cafeteria before making himself scarce. Jonny headed for the service area where a haggard woman was waiting to hand out roast beef sandwiches and bottles of water. It smelled wonderful and he eagerly accepted his plate.

Only when he'd settled at an empty table and eaten half the sandwich did Jonny realize that Asterion had used magic. He looked like a man, though with magic you could never tell for certain. Assuming illusion magic wasn't involved, that meant he had to be one of the hellpriests Conryu was fighting.

Jonny's next bite of sandwich went down hard. His last encounter with a hellpriest wasn't that long ago and he wasn't eager to repeat the experience.

A tournament to the death overseen by a hellpriest in an arena he knew not where. Great. He was a soldier. He was trained to kill the enemy and these people certainly qualified. The fact that he'd never actually killed someone might be a problem. Just thinking about it made him queasy. Since he didn't want to die here, he'd have to get over it, quickly.

Still, the idea of killing for the amusement of some rich assholes rubbed him the wrong way. If he could avoid it, he would. If not, well, then he'd do what he had to. No way was he dying here.

Jonny swallowed a sigh. He had a bad habit of stepping in shit, but this time, it seemed, he'd sunk in up to his ears.

5

After their meeting with Mr. Kane, Conryu and Maria left his office and made their way through the halls of the Department. Most people ignored them, though Prime drew a few looks. Conryu wasn't officially part of the team and the regular agents weren't sure how to treat him, therefore they ignored him.

He held Maria's hand as they walked, casually, but it was nice to know he could touch Maria like this without fear of hurting her. It was one of the great joys in his sometimes dark life. He was tempted to walk slower just to prolong their time together, but the situation didn't allow it. When they reached the lobby, Conryu blew out a long breath.

"I fear this is where we part company. Yesterday was great. I hope once we get this business settled, we can take some time together."

Maria smiled, but it struck him as melancholy. "I'd love that, but we both know that for the foreseeable future, you're on call for any and all threats. A day here and there is probably the best we can hope for."

She was right, damn the universe. "Yeah, I know. But it's nice to pretend once in a while. Is there any chance I can get you to gather everything the Department has on the gym where Jonny went missing and Big Bob? I need to make a couple stops before getting started."

"Not a problem. Everything should be in the case file. Want me to call you when I have it?"

"I'm going to be out of range. I'll call you when I'm set. Thanks for the help."

"Anytime. Do you actually have a plan?"

"I have an idea that, depending on my resources, might work. Might. Much as I'd like to just barge in, magic blazing, this is Central, not the middle of nowhere. I think a more subtle approach is called for."

She raised an eyebrow.

"What? I can be subtle."

Maria kissed his cheek. "As long as you come back alive and unharmed, I don't care if you burn the whole miserable city down. Love you."

"Love you too."

Maria headed back to the bank of elevators on the rear wall and Conryu strode through the front revolving door.

"What now, Master?" Prime asked.

Conryu opened a hell portal and walked through. Kai was waiting as always and she offered a little bow. A moment later Cerberus came trotting up, all three tongues swinging. Conryu patted his flank and Cerberus gave a happy bark.

"I need to talk to Kanna. Once I hear what she has to say, I'll decide my next move."

"Is there something I can do?" Kai asked, ever eager to be of service.

"Unfortunately, you won't work for what I have in mind, Kai. I'm not sure if any of the Daughters will, but I figured Kanna would know for sure."

Kai's eyes narrowed ever so slightly, but she would never question him. That was both nice and troublesome. Unless he was doing something obviously suicidal, she wouldn't argue. That didn't make her the best person to bounce ideas off of. On the plus side, knowing she'd never betray him made her perfect for watching his back.

Conryu flew up onto Cerberus and Kai joined him a moment later, wrapping her arms around his chest. He could've just willed them to the ancient monastery that the Daughters had converted into their base, but Cerberus seemed to enjoy carrying him and riding on the demon dog was fun. In this line of work, you found your pleasure where you could.

"Okay, boy. Take us to Kanna."

Cerberus barked once and leapt forward. Then they were racing through Hell's endless darkness. At least it felt like they were. When all was darkness, it was hard to tell.

The trip ended in seconds. Conryu flew down, gave Cerberus a parting pat on his central head, and opened a portal. He stepped out into the monastery courtyard. A dozen ninjas were sparring, while three more were practicing with shuriken.

Every one of them stopped what they were doing, took a knee, and stared at him. This sort of worshipful behavior happened often enough that he'd more or less gotten used to it. There was no point in telling them not to do it, since that seemed to be one of the few orders they were incapable of following.

"Chosen?" He turned to find Kanna emerging from the long stone building that served as their barracks. "How may we serve?"

"I've got kind of a weird situation and I'm hoping you'll know the right person to help me sort it out. Is there somewhere we can talk, just the two of us?"

As soon as he spoke, every ninja in the yard vanished into the borderland, leaving Kanna and Conryu alone.

"Right, that works I guess."

"Tell me about this problem, Chosen, and I will do my best to help."

Conryu ambled over and sat on the barracks' front step. Since she couldn't very well be standing over him, Kanna sat beside him. Just as he knew she would.

"Okay, here's the deal. I need a ninja with a particular build. Curvier than usual. Big boobs, nice butt, the sort of woman that will make a man's eyes pop out of his head. She needs to get a guy alone so I can talk to him with no one else around. And no one can know about it, that's why I'm not just grabbing the clown."

Kanna brought her hand to her chin. "This is, I will admit, not the sort of help I was expecting you to need. As assassins, we have some training in seduction techniques—not that we often have a chance to practice. And your description is also difficult. Most of the girls are quite slim thanks to all their training."

As she muttered, Conryu looked closer at Kanna herself. The black ninja uniform wasn't revealing, but it did fit snugly enough to show the curves underneath. Kanna just about fit the bill.

"I'm sorry, Chosen, I..." She noticed how closely he was looking at her and her eyes grew very wide. "You can't be thinking what I think you're thinking."

"Yup. You're the perfect woman for this job, Kanna."

"Surely one of the younger—"

Conryu shook his head. "You're young and pretty enough. Relax, you won't have to sleep with him or anything. Just get him to take you back to his place, or a back alley, or the bathroom for all I care. I just need him alone for five minutes. As soon as he answers my questions, I'll give him a memory of a night he'll never forget and we'll split."

"If that is your command, Chosen, then so be it. I'll leave one of the more experienced Daughters in charge while I'm gone."

"Perfect. I'll meet you in the borderland. We'll need to swing by a store and get you a new outfit, then I'll call Maria and see where we can find Big Bob."

"Big Bob?"

"Don't ask. See you in a minute."

Conryu opened a hell portal and strode through. He had total confidence that Kanna could do the job, though she'd need to loosen up about a thousand percent.

"Chosen, are you really going to make the grandmaster do this?" Kai asked. "I would be happy to take her place, as would any of the others."

"You're a lovely woman, Kai, but if Big Bob is anything like I think he'll be, you lack the assets to really get his attention. Kanna's borderline too slim, but she has more to work with than you or any of the other girls. With the right outfit, I'm confident she'll get the job done."

"I pity the Daughters not on assignment. Her training is going to be especially tough after this."

"It's just another mission," Conryu insisted. "Kanna will handle it like the professional she is."

Their conversation ended when the subject herself appeared. "I am ready, Chosen." She sounded like she was getting ready to go into battle with an army of demons.

"Great. I won't even make you ride on Cerberus."

The demon dog let out a little whine. Seemed Conryu couldn't please anyone today.

With an effort of will, Conryu shifted them to the Central shopping district. He was about to open a portal then stopped. They couldn't very well walk into a shop with Kanna dressed like a ninja. Someone was liable to call for a padded wagon.

"Quick change of plans. We need to get you some civilian clothes before we go shopping. You're about Shizuku's size. We can pick up something at Maria's place."

"Will Maria's mother not object to you borrowing something from her closet?" Kai asked.

"Nah, I'll return it to Maria with an explanation after we get Kanna her new outfit."

A moment later they were standing in the Kanes' empty apartment, the master bedroom to be specific. Conryu gestured at the

JAMES E WISHER

walk-in closet on the far side of a king-sized bed. "Pick something out and get changed. I'll wait in the living room."

"What do you wish me to wear?" Kanna asked.

"Something that doesn't scream 'deadly assassin.' Other than that, your choice. Kai, help her out."

"Me? I know nothing about clothes."

"You're both women. I'm sure once the closet door opens, your instincts will kick in. Just don't make a mess." Conryu stepped into the living room with Prime at his shoulder then closed the door. "Those two might be the only women I've ever met that aren't interested in clothes."

"The forge in Black City is probably more to their liking," Prime said.

"No doubt." Conryu pulled out his phone and dialed Maria. "Hey. Did you get the intel for me?"

"Yeah, all set. Want me to read it or e-mail it to you?"

"E-mail. By the way, I'm at your place. One of the ninjas needed some civilian clothes and she's the same size as your mom, more or less. We're borrowing one of her outfits. Would you let her know for me?"

"Sure, but you really should've asked first. Mom wouldn't have minded."

"I know, but I wanted to have everything ready for tonight and if she's busy I would've had to interrupt. This seemed easier."

Maria blew out a long sigh. "The e-mail is on its way and I'll smooth things over with Mom. Be careful tonight. I read Big Bob's file. He's a nasty customer, under suspicion of several murders, though there's insufficient evidence to bring him in."

"I just fought a hellpriest like three weeks ago. However tough this clown is, I doubt he's that tough. I'll have Kai and Kanna with me, so no need to worry. I'll be in touch when I have more news."

He disconnected just as Kanna emerged from the bedroom dressed in a black dress that ended about knee high and hugged her curves very nicely. With the mask gone, he got a clear look at her pale, heart-shaped face; small, upturned nose; and full red lips. Only the deep frown spoiled the image.

"You look gorgeous. Any doubt I had about whether or not you were right for the job has been washed away. You're perfect."

Maybe she'd never been complimented on her looks before. He didn't know, but from the slight blush that formed on her cheeks when he fell silent, he decided she seemed pleased. The frown even eased a fraction.

"I'm pleased you're satisfied, Chosen. What now?"

"My original plan was to go somewhere and get you a properly slutty outfit, but having seen you in Mrs. Kane's dress, I'm tempted to just let you stay the way you are."

Conryu studied Kanna and tapped his chin. She really did look stunning, but also innocent. Would someone like Big Bob be drawn to that or would a more wanton look work better? Conryu had never been much of a partier, so he had little more experience at this sort of thing than the ninjas did.

"Chosen, when you look at me so frankly, it's a bit uncomfortable."

"Sorry, I was lost in thought. Seducing a fight promoter isn't exactly in my wheelhouse." Conryu slapped his forehead. "I know the perfect person to ask. Just a second."

He opened a hell portal. "Dark Lady."

It took a few seconds, but his beautiful succubus agent finally emerged from the portal. She had bat wings, curves for days, and wore the sexy biker-chic outfit he made for her not that long ago.

As soon as she saw him she smiled in a way that would've melted a lesser man's knees. "Master, it's been so long. I missed you."

Before he could say anything, she hugged him, pressing her outrageous figure against him.

He disentangled himself as quickly as possible. He loved Maria more than anything, but he was still only human. Too much of that might break his will. "Things have been hectic. I have a very small job for you. This is Kanna, Grandmaster of the Daughters of the Reaper."

The Dark Lady raised a perfectly curved eyebrow at that.

"I know, I know. She's going undercover." Conryu quickly explained the situation. "Anyway, you're the expert. Do you think this outfit or something a bit sluttier?"

"Sluttier for sure. You need to make him an offer he can't refuse." The Dark Lady walked once around Kanna, studying her from every angle. By the time she was done, Kanna's face had turned bright red. "She's got the looks, but why not just have me do it?"

"Excellent idea," Kanna said.

"Afraid not. Big Bob is certain to have at least one wizard for protection. She'd spot a demon, even a disguised one, in a blink. It's got to be someone human."

"You do know that Kanna gives off a faint aura of corruption," the Dark Lady said.

In fact, Conryu hadn't known that, but after the power boost he gave her during his time filling in for the Reaper, he wasn't shocked. "I have a way to deal with it. Here's your mission. Take Kanna shopping and give her some pointers. I have no doubt that after a few hours of your tutelage, she'll be able to seduce a dead man."

The Dark Lady beamed. "You always say the sweetest things, Master."

Conryu ushered them through the hell portal and out of the Kanes' living room. "I'll drop you two in the shopping district. Kai and I will check out the Fists of Steel gym. When you're finished, meet us in the borderland."

"As you command, Chosen." Kanna spoke like a woman about to embark on a death march.

Conryu had never been shopping with a demon, but it couldn't be that bad, right?

6

Jonny sat by himself at a long wooden table in the cafeteria. He'd finished one roast beef sandwich and was about halfway through a second. The accommodations might be rough, but at least the food tasted good. If he died tomorrow, it wouldn't be of hunger.

No, damn it! He had to stop thinking that way!

He glanced around at the other fighters. Most were still eating and none of them were talking. Pretty hard to get friendly with someone you might be forced to kill down the road. Of course, given what he'd seen since going undercover, most of the fighters tended to be on the antisocial side. That's what made getting information out of them so difficult.

His gloomy thoughts were interrupted when the cafeteria doors opened and Loong entered carrying a stack of paper. "The tournament draw has been determined. If you're interested, come get a copy."

Jonny hopped to his feet and trotted over. He was the first to arrive and take his paper from the perpetually scowling Loong. A few of the others made their way over with a good deal less haste, but Jonny ignored them and returned to his seat.

It was a pretty simple bracket. Everyone had a number and you were paired up based on that. Jonny winced when he found his name. Number thirty-two, bottom of the barrel. Which meant he was paired with number one, supposedly the best fighter in the group. Not exactly ideal.

Oddly, there was another number beside every name but his. What was the point of that? His opponent, Lala Ozkin—Jonny shook his head at that name—had the number six beside his.

As he racked his brain trying to figure out what the number meant on the off chance it was important, the faint scuff of approaching footsteps drew his attention. He looked up just as a swarthy man with broad shoulders and a bare, heavily muscled chest stopped across from him. His head was shaved smooth and a curling mustache decorated his upper lip.

"Greeting!" The new arrival flashed a set of yellow-stained teeth. "May I join you?"

Seeing no reason to be rude, Jonny said, "Sure. Everyone else seems to be keeping their distance from each other so I didn't expect company."

"It is a difficult situation indeed. But I have always been the gregarious sort. My name is Lala Ozkin and I will be murdering you in the arena tomorrow. Please don't let that stand in the way of us being friends in the meantime."

Jonny stared at the man, his brain refusing to process what he'd just been told. After a few seconds he said, "Are you crazy?"

Lala threw back his head and laughed. Every pair of eyes in the place turned to look at him.

When he got himself under control Lala said, "You are not the first person to ask me that. I have had a difficult life, filled with toil and suffering. Knowing any day may be my last, I have chosen to live life to the fullest, enjoying every moment. I hate no man, even one I'm about to kill. And should you by some miracle defeat me tomorrow, my soul will bear you no grudge."

"That's very broad-minded of you. Rest assured that if you kill me, my soul will haunt you until the end of time."

Lala laughed again. "You have a good sense of humor. I wish we had some raki to toast our new friendship, but alas, our dour keeper says that drinking is not allowed. Perhaps he fears it will be bad for our health."

More guffaws followed the lame joke. Jonny couldn't fully suppress the faint smile that curled his lips. "Quick question. Do you know what the numbers after all the names save mine mean?"

"Yes, that's how many of their earlier opponents a fighter killed. As you can see, I killed all six of mine. You, apparently, killed none of yours. I found that strange given what we're here to do."

"The guy running my entry tournament said killing wasn't necessary to win. The cops in Central look a lot harder for a murderer than they do someone that committed assault. I figured if I got arrested, I'd have a strong claim that we'd both agreed to get in the ring and therefore accepted the outcome of the fight. Pretty hard to argue I didn't kill someone when their corpse is lying in the morgue, likely with traces of my blood on his knuckles."

"I see you are a deep thinker. The woman running my entry tournament assured me that it didn't matter if I killed my opponents since she'd make the bodies disappear. That seems more practical given the situation."

"That depends how you look at it." Jonny was happy to keep the conversation going as it stopped him from thinking about the fight to come. "Big Bob is a full-time fight promoter with a small club that serves as a fight venue. If one of his guys gets hurt, he can be healed with magic and fighting for the crowd's pleasure in a few days. Killing productive assets is bad business."

"You know, that may be the difference. The woman overseeing my fights usually just runs a night club. We were a two-weekend special event. The killing actually seemed to excite her customers more. There are many sick people in the world."

For a moment, Jonny thought that was another of Lala's bad jokes, but the solemn expression made it clear that he meant it. It also implied that he didn't consider himself one of them.

They chatted about random odds and ends for another fifteen minutes before Loong announced, "The rest of the day is yours. There's a gym if you want to exercise, or you can hang out here or back in the barracks. Just behave yourselves. No fighting or other violence until tomorrow. Anyone breaking this rule will be removed from the tournament and forfeit any chance at the big chest of gold. Clear?"

When no one spoke, he nodded once and marched out of the cafeteria.

"He is very lacking in charm," Lala said.

Jonny nodded. "Pretty sure that's not a requirement for this sort of work."

"True. Pity though. I believe I'm going to indulge in some light lifting. Would you like to join me?"

Jonny pushed himself away from the table and stood. "Sure. One last question if you'll indulge me."

"Certainly, my friend. Ask what you will. My life is an open book."

He seemed to mean it, but Jonny still had trouble wrapping his mind around the odd fighter. "Don't you think it's going to be hard for us to fight tomorrow if we get to be friends today?"

"Why would it? Business is business after all. I feel no personal animosity toward any of the people I fight. I'm just doing my job. Do you feel differently?"

Jonny didn't know how to answer that. He hadn't felt anything in particular about the men he beat on his way here. It did help that they all seemed like dickheads in need of an ass-kicking. "I guess I never thought about it. We'll find out tomorrow though, won't we?"

Lala offered another great belly laugh at that. "Indeed we will. Come my friend, we have fed our bodies, now let us gather what extra strength we can. You never know what might be the difference."

That was certainly the truth. Jonny figured he'd need every bit of strength he could muster if he didn't want his new best friend to kill him.

7

Conryu studied the Fists of Steel gym through a viewing portal in Hell. It looked exactly like he'd expected: a little bit run-down, built out of gray cement blocks that no one had bothered to paint, and was situated in a rough neighborhood. His father's dojo this was not. It looked like the sort of place serious and desperate fighters went to learn how to become professionals.

All in all, he kind of liked it.

He glanced at Kai who stood, silent as always, as she waited for his orders. "What do you think?"

"It wouldn't be my first choice of places to exercise, Chosen."

"It's no rougher than the monastery the Daughters call home. But forget that for now. I'm going in to take a look around. I want you to check out the basement. Let me know if there's any sign of magic."

She bowed and gave the exact answer he expected. "Yes, Chosen."

Conryu opened a hell portal in an alley a block from the gym. He would've gotten closer, but all the other alleys were occupied by bums at the moment and he didn't want to give one of them a heart attack.

A simple spell rendered Prime invisible before Conryu ambled out of the alley and down the sidewalk, enjoying the summer breeze despite the hint of garbage it carried. The breeze frequently stank worse than that back home in Sentinel City. Was it strange that he still thought of Sentinel City as home? He hadn't lived there in over a year. Mom had let the apartment's lease lapse and made herself a new home in Central. As for Conryu, the closest thing he had to a home at this point was his rebuilt log cabin on the floating island. Not that he was there very often.

At the gym he paused and glanced up at the sign above the door. It depicted two men made of glowing neon, boxing. He tried the door and found it unlocked. With a shrug he walked in only to be slammed in the nose by the stink of sweaty bodies. The crash of weights hitting the floor mingled with the thud of fists on heavy bags.

He moved deeper into the building. No one greeted him, so he headed for the ring that dominated the center of the exercise floor. Two men were sparring while a dozen or so watched from the outside. When he got closer, one of the men, a lean bald fellow with skulls tattooed on his cheeks, noticed him.

Scowling, Skullcheeks stalked over. Conryu took a moment to study him as he did. Some sort of magic lingered in his mind. Clearly the man's memories had been tampered with. What he couldn't tell was whether anything else had been done to him.

There's a trigger imbedded in his mind, Master. I don't know exactly what it will do when activated, but I doubt it will be anything good.

Conryu bathed Skullcheeks's brain in a microburst of dark magic, making him sway like a drunk and shake his head.

Did I get it?

Yes, Master.

"You're new here," Skullcheeks said when he finally reached

Conryu. His eyes were a little glassy, but otherwise he seemed no worse for having his brain tampered with.

"Yes, sir," Conryu said. "I was looking for a place to work out. A buddy of mine that fights for Big Bob recommended this place."

"You seem like a nice kid, so I'll give you a free piece of advice. Stay away from Bob. He grinds fighters up and spits them out as broken husks of what they once were. Let your buddy know too."

"I appreciate the warning, but I need money and fighting seemed like a good way to get plenty of it in a hurry." Conryu looked around as if he were about to share a secret. "I heard a rumor that you sometimes host big-money fights in the basement. Any chance I can get in on that?"

Skullcheeks scrubbed a hand down his face, suddenly looking tired rather than angry. "I don't know who started that rumor, but I swear if I ever get my hands on them they'll curse their mother for giving birth to them. This joint might be a little rough, but I run an aboveboard business. I train fighters, damn good ones too. Two world champions in a decade. More than any other independent gym, I promise you that. I wish I could keep all my boys away from scum like Bob, but like you, there are always a few desperate enough to take the bait of easy money."

Conryu was rapidly revising his opinion of both Skullcheeks and his gym upward. It looked like he was just an unfortunate dupe that was used by whoever made off with Jonny and the other fighters. That was no doubt the memory that had been destroyed.

"I haven't made any promises or signed a contract or anything yet. Having heard what you said, I think I'll look for another way to make some cash."

Skullcheeks grinned. "Smart, kid. You want to work out here, you're welcome anytime."

"Thanks."

There was a loud crash and Skullcheeks spun and hurried back to the ring where one of the fighters had landed flat on his back, seemingly out cold.

Conryu ducked back out the door. He hadn't learned much beyond the fact that there were at least a few good people left in the world.

He retreated back to the empty alley, but before he could open a hell portal, Kai appeared. "The gym is being watched. After I checked the basement, I scouted the area and found a van. Inside were two wizards and a man in a gray suit tending some complex-looking computer equipment."

"That'll be the Department's team. As long as they don't get in my way, I'm content to leave them alone for the moment. Good catch, Kai. What about the basement?"

"I couldn't get in. A barrier blocked me from shifting."

"The Fists of Steel gym gets more interesting by the moment. Let's catch up with Kanna and the Dark Lady. Maybe Big Bob can give us some more insights."

———

Dominic McCoy had never held any particularly strong feelings with regard to the so-called druids that lived in the Cascade Forest. They did their thing and for the most part left the modern world alone. Big deal. Yet for some reason he found himself bouncing his way up a rutted trail that would have to be considerably improved to be called a road. At the end of the trail waited the druids' camp. The same camp he'd visited less than a month ago and found nothing.

Maybe it was a test. The higher-ups did all kinds of crazy stuff. Sending him and his easily irritated partner, Lois, out for a second look wouldn't be the strangest thing he'd heard of in his six years with the Department.

Annoying or not, as long as his paycheck cleared, Dom would drive Lois up here as many times as he was ordered to.

A quick glance at his partner's scowling, wrinkled face made it clear she was less sanguine about their current assignment. He was tempted to make a joke about her face freezing like that if she wasn't careful, but since Dom didn't want his ass set on fire, he refrained.

"Did they tell you anything they didn't tell me?" Dom asked.

"What did they tell you?" Lois asked.

"Basically drive up here and take another look around."

"Seems a civilian wizard detected a burst of dark magic from the general vicinity of the camp and called it in. When he called me into his office, Senior Agent Anders made it pretty clear that he thought we screwed the job up last time and we'd best not do so this time." Lois snarled. "This clown, who's never wielded magic in his life, gives me a dressing-down like I screwed up. I searched that collection of shacks from one end to the other and didn't find so much as a spark of dark magic. You saw me!"

Dom nodded. He had, indeed, seen her walk around doing whatever it was that wizards did. Whether she missed something or not, he couldn't say and wouldn't dare say even if he could.

"Do you think it's a test?"

"If it is, it's the dumbest, most pointless test in the history of testing. I'm a twenty-year veteran. I know what I'm doing and if I say there's no dark magic in that collection of shacks, then there isn't."

"Maybe there wasn't then, but there is now." They hit a particularly deep rut, bouncing Dom off the seat a few inches. "I haven't been at this as long as you, but if there's one thing I've figured out, it's that where magic is concerned, things can change in a hurry."

Her snarling visage softened. "That's surprisingly insightful. Perhaps I underestimated you."

That was as close as he ever hoped to get to a compliment from Lois, so Dom smiled and fell silent, content to take the win. They were getting close to the camp anyway. He had to focus. On the off chance that one of the nuts jumped out at them again, he'd just as soon not have to fill out all the paperwork that came with running someone over.

A few minutes later they drove into the camp, or at least what used to be the camp. It looked like a tornado had hit the place. The shacks were torn apart and their remains scattered around the clearing. Even the earth had been gouged open. Of the druids, he saw no sign.

Dom had never encountered anything like the mess in front of him. Clearly the bosses hadn't sent them on a wild-goose chase this time.

Lois hopped out of the SUV and strode around the clearing while Dom kept his distance. His hand strayed to the grip of his pistol, but there was nothing to shoot. In fact, he had serious doubts that a bullet would bother whatever did this.

"I'm sensing residual dark magic, which means that whatever spell got reported was high level. The lack of bodies makes me think the druids were fully consumed by the magic."

Dom scratched his head. The kooks had lived here for decades, why did someone choose now to wipe them out? He hadn't heard anything about them causing trouble and even if they did, the loggers that were their usual targets would come after them with guns, not high-level magic.

"What do you make of it?" Dom asked at last.

"I don't know. But you can bet it was nothing good. We'd best get back and report in. Anders isn't going to like this."

Dom didn't like it and he only had the barest idea what was going on. Times like these made him glad he was an agent with no particular authority. Dealing with crazy shit like this had to be bad for your sanity.

8

M iguel tightened his grip on the vine that kept him secure on the back of the giant bird creature Malice had created. They'd been traveling south nonstop since leaving the druid village. Below them the scenery was little more than a blur that changed color depending on whether they were over land or water. Miguel had never moved so fast for so long. He assumed he had the power to do something like this as well, but lacked the knowledge. Considering she hadn't spoken a word to him since taking her place right behind the creature's long neck, Malice was clearly in no rush to relieve his ignorance.

At least the wind blew away the worst of the bird's stench. It reeked of rotting vegetation and dead flesh. Not surprising since that's what it was made of, but hardly pleasant all the same.

He didn't even know where they were going. When he'd asked a few hours after they set out, he'd been roundly ignored. He was supposed to be the Chosen of Baphomet, yet this demon, or whatever she was, acted like he was little more than an annoyance to be humored, not a master to be obeyed. Even though they were supposed to be on the same side, he found he'd begun to hate her for that. Since he'd gotten a taste of power, his tolerance for disrespect had dropped.

The problem for him remained unchanged. He lacked the power or skill to do anything about it. Until that changed, he'd remain irrelevant. One way or another it *would* change.

He'd barely settled in to brood over his current situation when the bird started to descend. They were directly over the ocean and the water was coming up fast.

Malice gave a little shiver and the next thing Miguel knew they were floating on a mat of rotten vines ripped from the bird's back. Their transport crashed into the water and quickly sank out of sight under the waves. They flew much more slowly toward a nearby beach where Malice set them down.

"Why did you destroy it?" Miguel asked. "That creature might have been of use to us down the road."

"It was used up. I pumped magic into it the whole way here to maximize speed. In the process the rotting accelerated. It would've fallen apart on its own in under an hour."

"Where are we?"

"About ten miles north of Santa Angeles."

"And why are we heading toward the largest city on the West Coast?"

"I can access information and resources there. Things I used to control when I was still alive. We need to know what's going on in the world before we can plan our next move. Knowledge is nearly as important as the power to use it."

"Why didn't you just tell me all that when I asked you the first time?" Miguel asked, some of his annoyance leaking into his voice despite his best efforts to remain under control.

Malice's wrinkly face got even wrinklier when she frowned. "When did you ask me?"

"A little while after we took off. You just ignored the question."

"I didn't even hear you. To make the trip as quickly as possible, I merged my consciousness with the bird. My entire focus was on getting us as close to the city as I could before the rotten mass totally fell apart."

Miguel's cheeks burned as he realized that once again his ignorance had been exposed. "You should explain these things before you begin."

"If I have to explain every move I make before I make it, we'll be forever getting Baphomet's mission completed. You've spoken to the demon lord more than I have. Surely you understand that he isn't the most patient being."

He had, indeed, come to that conclusion as well. "Fair enough, but I want regular updates at least. Starting right now with our immediate plans."

"We have a few hours until dark. Let's find somewhere out of sight and I'll tell you what I have in mind."

Now that her mind was no longer connected to the bird construct, Malice seemed a good deal more attentive to his requirements. Perhaps he'd simply misjudged her and let his ego and impatience get the better of him.

Miguel smiled, feeling much better about the situation. He and Malice would work together and nothing, not even the Reaper's Chosen, would keep them from claiming this world for Baphomet.

Malice strode along behind the idiot hellpriest Baphomet had saddled her with. The boy clearly knew nothing of any use. But he did have considerable power; all she needed to do was figure out how to control him and thus gain access to it. For the moment, playing along and letting him think she gave even the tiniest fraction of a damn what he thought about her plans seemed the best course. Like all men with power, he needed his ego stroked a bit.

She hated having to make the effort. When she was alive, even the most powerful men rushed to do her bidding. Well, all but one of them at least.

Her lips twisted in a snarl when she pictured the face of the one that killed her. Conryu Koda would suffer greatly for that insult. Eventually. When she'd gathered her power, molded the idiot into something useful, and made every preparation possible, then and only then would Malice strike.

When she looked down at the sand her expression smoothed. Though she still looked like her old self, the pain was gone. She could move freely, untroubled by arthritis and the many other illnesses that had ravaged her nearly dead body. Even if she got nothing else out of this arrangement, the chance to walk on Earth one more time free from pain was a great gift. Not that Malice had any intention of settling for such a minor reward.

The idiot, what was his name? He'd said it once she felt certain. Morris? No, Miguel, that was it. Miguel was headed for the shadow of a towering rock face. It was a good spot to wait for nightfall. That he'd picked it out on his own raised her opinion of him by the tiniest of fractions.

Miguel sat with his back to the stone and looked up at her. Though Malice felt no fatigue in her new body, she didn't want to loom over him either. Now wasn't the time to assert dominance. Should he lash out blindly, he did have raw power enough to possibly send her back to Baphomet's hell. Malice seriously doubted she'd get a warm reception should she return before completing her task.

So she sat in the sand and sighed.

"It's nice here," Miguel said. "Reminds me of home. But I'm sure you don't care about that. Tell me the plan."

He was certainly right about Malice's indifference to his home. "For the moment I want to access Kincade Industries' West Coast headquarters. There's a massive magical library as well as a computer network tied in to everything. One night there should give us all the information we need to make long-term plans. My hope is that a mothballed project of mine might be resurrected to provide us with high-quality hosts for Baphomet's thralls."

"We need seeds from a Black Eternal, but I lost both of the ones I had. Summoning minor demonic spirits one at a time takes too long."

"Our lord told me of these plants. We're not in that huge of a rush, but you're correct, we will eventually need at least one Black Eternal. For now, information and a base will be a good start."

"You speak of this place we're going as if you're very familiar with it."

"Of course I'm familiar with it. In life I ran the company. I know every nook and cranny, every dirty secret, and where all the bodies are buried."

He stared at her as if not fully comprehending what she was saying. "Do you not recognize the name Malice Kincade?"

Miguel shook his head. "We had very little in the way of technology where I grew up and during my brief visit to Miami, I didn't have time to investigate the business district. I take it the company is a large one?"

"Kincade Industries is the largest, most powerful company in the world. We have our fingers in every pie, so to speak."

"I was a fisherman struggling not to starve to death." Miguel heaved a great sigh and shrugged. "And now you're dead and I'm a hellpriest. It seems both our lives have changed."

"Indeed." Malice shifted a bit to look out over the ocean. The sunset was coloring the ocean bloodred and she found that a promising omen. "If I provide the mental image, can you transport us both to the campus?"

"Certainly." The idiot looked pleased to have something to do, just as she'd hoped. "Did you know that there are tiny plants pretty much everywhere? I can sense them and anywhere they are, I can transport us."

"Splendid. I was certain I could count on you. As soon as true night falls, we'll make our move."

"Why wait?" Miguel asked.

"At night there's only a skeleton crew of guards on the campus. Since we're not looking to draw attention, leaving a few dozen bodies lying around wouldn't be prudent."

His eyes widened. "Is that why you used the dead druids in your construct?"

That had very little to do with it, but she nodded as if he'd guessed something important. "Exactly. Though we are strong, we're far from ready to take on the strongest. If he finds us before the time is right, we'll both end up in Baphomet's hell facing our master's wrath."

Miguel shuddered. Good, at least he was smart enough to understand exactly how bad that would be.

Malice waited a full hour before she stood and said, "It's time."

Miguel scrambled to his feet and hurried over. "I've never done this using someone else's visualization. What do I need to do?"

"Nothing different from what you'd normally do. Relax and when the image appears, take us there just like it was your own thought." Malice had always pitied the Academy teachers, turned out she was right to do so.

"I'm ready."

Malice seriously doubted that, but time was wasting. She pictured the campus, specifically the green where employees could spend their lunch hour should they need a break from their computers. It was rich with growing things and so should be the easiest place for them to arrive. When the image was clear in her mind, she insinuated it into Miguel's.

"I have it. Hold on."

Black vines shot up and wrapped around her. There was darkness and the sensation of movement. Malice vaguely saw dirt all around her. It felt like they were actually passing through the earth. And maybe they were. This specific ability was totally new to her.

A few seconds later the vines unwrapped and they were standing in a garbage-filled alley across from the campus. Couldn't the fool even complete this task without fouling it up?

Taking a moment to calm herself, Malice said, "This isn't where we're supposed to be."

"I know, but I hit a wall and couldn't get through. This was the next place I could find that seemed safe to appear."

"Hmm. So someone added a barrier around the entire campus. Recently too, since I didn't give the order." She shrugged. "We'll have to go in the front door then. Not ideal, but a little transformation magic and no one will recognize us."

"I thought this was your business. Can't you order them to let us in?"

"As far as everyone knows, I'm dead, remember? Galling as it is, I no longer have any authority here."

"Then we'll have to force our way in."

"It may come to that, but I haven't been dead for long. If my access codes haven't been revoked, we may yet get in quietly." Malice didn't hold out a ton of hope. Kincade security had always been top-notch. "Hold still."

Since she could no longer use illusion magic, Malice was forced to take a roundabout way to create their disguises. She gathered earth around them and shaped it first into masks that looked like perfectly human faces and then into pads that would change their body shape so that anyone looking at a recording wouldn't recognize them. It was a crude process, but should be adequate for her purposes. Once she gained access to the central computer, shutting down all the cameras would be a simple matter. Then they'd be free to go about their business without concern.

With the masks and pads in place, she led the way across the street to the closed steel gate that barred entry to the campus. The guard shack was empty at night, but there was a number pad that would allow anyone with the correct access code to enter at any time, day or night.

Mentally crossing her fingers, Malice punched in her old code. Just as she feared, the screen flashed once and a buzzer sounded, indicating failure. She didn't try again. A second failure would alert security, exactly what she wanted to avoid.

Hopefully a little dark magic would do the trick. If it didn't, more drastic measures would be necessary. Concentrating on the delicate electronics, Malice inserted a thin stream of dark magic directly into the console. Wires and connections decayed and a moment later sparks shot out and the gate clicked loose.

"It's open. Would you mind pulling it the rest of the way?"

Miguel grabbed the gate and yanked. And nearly ended up on his backside for his trouble as the gate slid open effortlessly and silently. Good to see maintenance remained every bit as efficient as security.

"You could've warned me," Miguel said as they slipped inside and hurried toward the largest building.

"I didn't think you'd just pull with all your might. A good rule of thumb that applies to both magic and mundane matters is never use more power than absolutely necessary. It's a waste of time and wears you out."

Miguel scowled. "With Baphomet's power at my command, I don't wear out easily."

Looked like a bit more ego stroking was needed. "Of course not, but teaching you magical best practices is part of my task. Whether you choose to follow them is entirely up to you."

His expression smoothed, exactly as she'd hoped. Manipulating the boy took almost no effort for her. After so many years of practice, she did it without much thought.

"What now?" he asked when they reached the heavy glass door of the main building.

She held a finger to her lips and repeated the process she'd used on the first control pad. The results were happily the same and she pulled the door open and slipped inside the dark, silent lobby. Unless things had changed, there should be eight two-man guard patrols roaming the floors. With their magic, evasion shouldn't be an issue. Especially since the central computer was on the first floor.

Malice led the way through the lobby and out a door that led deeper into the building. All her senses were alert for any sign of danger. Danger of detection, not harm. The overworked, under-paid rent-a-cops they used for security had no more hope of hurting Malice than a cockroach did.

Fortunately, they encountered no one before reaching the room Malice sought. This one, of course, also had a keypad that needed destroying. It yielded as easily as the first two and Malice pushed her way into the building's command center.

A wall of monitors directly ahead greeted her. A quick study indicated that the guards were all on higher levels. Good.

She sat in front of one of the computers and started typing.

"What should I do?" Miguel asked.

"Watch the monitors." Malice pointed to one in particular. "That's the hall outside. If you see any guards coming, let me know. I shouldn't be long, then we can move on to the library."

"Why does a business have a library?"

"Magical reference books. Kincade Industries specializes in mass-produced magical items and the wizards need them for research."

He fell mercifully silent after that, allowing Malice to work in peace. First, she called up the main menu. As soon as she saw it she froze. At the top it listed the company executives and at the very top it said, Kelsie Kincade, President and CEO. Why was her granddaughter listed as running the company? Cassandra was still years away from retirement and Malice seriously doubted Kelsie had what it took to run the company anyway.

She shook her head. It didn't matter. Let the useless brat run the company into the ground. Malice was long past caring. If nothing else, having someone incompetent in charge would make her own work easier.

Clicking deeper into the system, she found the facility she needed and confirmed that it was still shut down. Good. If no one had done anything with it in ten years, maybe they'd all forgotten about it. That would suit her very well.

Leaving that page, she clicked over to the library catalogue. There were some reference books she wanted and hopefully they'd have them here. If not, she wasn't sure where she'd find them.

Luck was with her once again and this facility had a number of books on the subject. On the downside, she had to access the library computer for more details.

Her final task was to shut down the recording system so they could move around without the disguises. That done, she stood. "All clear?"

"Yes. The nearest guards are on the third floor and slowly making their way down."

"Perfect. The library is in the basement."

Malice smiled to herself as she led the way to the basement stairs. If the books contained the information she needed, then very soon Baphomet would learn just how foolish it was to underestimate Malice Kincade.

9

K anna had said on many occasions that the Daughters of the Reaper stood ready to do whatever the Chosen required. When she said it, she'd meant that they would kill or die for him. She looked in the mirror at the ridiculous dress the Dark Lady had forced her to put on. It had more holes than dress, barely covered her ass, and left the tops of her breasts exposed for anyone to see. Though her usual uniform offered no special protection, for some reason she found this outfit left her feeling more vulnerable.

The dressing room door opened, revealing the Dark Lady in all her feminine perfection. She wore the outfit the Chosen had made for her, denim shorts, a t-shirt that left her middle bare, and a pair of thigh-high leather boots.

The demon looked her up and down, nodded once, and said, "Perfect. No man with a pulse will be able to resist you. Why do you look so glum? This is a chance to serve him directly. Don't you lot live for that sort of thing?"

"We're warriors, not..." Kanna trailed off and made a disgusted gesture at her outfit. "This."

The Dark Lady cocked her head. "My understanding was that

you were whatever he needed you to be. Tonight you're going to be bait. Maybe next week you'll kidnap someone or fight an enemy wizard. That's the job."

"I understand my responsibilities, but that does not mean I have to be happy about it."

"At least try not to look so miserable. You know if he sees you with that expression he'll feel bad. It's also hard to seduce someone when everything below the neck says one thing and your face says, 'I want to kill you as slowly and painfully as possible.'"

Kanna forced her expression back to neutral and nodded. The demon was right. If one of her subordinates had acted this way on a mission, she'd have given the girl a thorough dressing-down. She would complete the task the Chosen had given her. Her honor demanded nothing less.

"That's better, but when you approach the target, you'll want something like this." The Dark Lady lowered her head a little so she was looking through her eyelashes, a mysterious smile playing around her lips. Her tongue slowly licked them and she smiled wider. "Get the idea?"

"I believe so. Let's pay for this torn rag you call a dress and get out of here."

"That's the spirit."

The pair wove their way through the racks of clothes, most of them just as scandalous as what Kanna wore. The eyes of every woman in the place followed them with burning envy. Whatever else you might say about her, the Dark Lady clearly knew her business.

At the checkout counter, a young lady with purple hair and more piercings than Kanna had time to count scanned the tag still on the back of her dress. The Dark Lady paid with money the Chosen had provided.

When the clerk handed her back her change she said, "You ladies are going to be very popular at the clubs. Maybe I'll see you tonight."

The Dark Lady winked. "Maybe."

Outside the shop, they ducked into an empty alley and Kanna shifted them both to the borderland. As soon as the endless darkness surrounded them, she let out a long sigh. Here, at least, no one would be looking at her.

"You need to work on your flirting," the Dark Lady said. "That purple-haired girl was itching for some attention from you."

Kanna stared for a moment. "I didn't notice."

"Exactly, that's what you need to work on. If she'd wanted to kill you, you'd have sensed it right away."

"Of course, that's what I'm trained for. I think you're reading too much into this mission. I doubt it will be a task I must perform regularly." At least Kanna fervently hoped that would be the case.

She sensed an approaching presence and a moment later spotted Cerberus carrying Kai and the Chosen toward them. Kanna tensed then forced herself to relax. This was the moment of truth. Hopefully he would be pleased by her sacrifice.

The Chosen hopped down, gave her one look, and whistled. "Wow. Big Bob doesn't stand a chance."

"I'm happy you're pleased, Chosen," Kanna said.

"I'll be even more pleased if this clown has the information I need. We checked out the gym and there's definitely something fishy going on there. Kai found a barrier in the basement that kept her from entering and the owner's memories had been altered."

"Why not just force your way in and see what's there?" Kanna asked.

"That's a last-resort option, but I prefer not to do anything that might put Jonny in danger, at least not until we exhaust our other avenues." He turned to the Dark Lady. "You did a great job, thanks."

He floated over and kissed her on the cheek. The creature

actually blushed. Kanna wouldn't have believed the shameless demon capable of such a reaction.

"Always a pleasure to serve, Master. If there's nothing else, I'll return to Black City."

"I think we're all set. Until next time."

The Dark Lady vanished into the darkness and Kanna found herself alone with Kai and the Chosen. He was awfully close and she didn't have nearly as many clothes on as she'd prefer.

"Okay, here's the plan." If he was aware of her discomfort, he took mercy on her and showed no sign of it. "I got the intel on Big Bob from Maria. He hangs out at a club called The Pit. I'm sure it's every bit as nice as it sounds. It got the name because of a fighting pit where matches are held. You're going to go in like a regular patron, find Big Bob, and lure him somewhere. Kai and I will be watching from the borderland, so no need to worry about anything going badly."

A gesture from him conjured an image of a massive, bald black man dressed in a navy suit.

"Big Bob?" Kanna asked.

"Bingo." The Chosen snapped his fingers. "Almost forgot."

He pulled his boot off then his sock and handed her the tiny ring that had been on his little toe. "That will absorb your excess dark magic. I'll need it back when you're done. Maria and I can't get close without it."

"It will be safe with me, Chosen." Kanna removed her right shoe and slipped the ring on. She felt no different afterwards, but assumed it was doing what it was supposed to.

"Prime?"

"She's good, Master," the scholomantic said. "No one would ever guess she was anything but a normal woman."

The Chosen shook his head. "Only a blind man would mistake her for a normal woman, but I take your point. By the way, where's Shizuku's dress? I need to drop it off with Maria."

Kanna winced. "I fear I forgot it at the store. Apologies, Chosen."

"No worries. What was the name of the store? We'll pick it up on our way to The Pit."

Kanna stared at him as she racked her brain. At last she was forced to admit that she had no idea. Her mind had been so clouded by worries that she hadn't been paying proper attention to her surroundings. A first-year Daughter would've done a better job than her.

"It's okay." He whispered something and blew a puff of air across his palm. "I asked the Dark Lady to let one of the Daughters know and have her pick it up."

"Thank you, Chosen." She offered a bow, not as low as was proper, but given her outfit, as low as she dared go.

No more mistakes. From here on, she would complete her mission flawlessly.

Conryu opened a portal a block from The Pit and Kanna stepped out. He wished he could've gotten closer given the horrid high-heeled shoes the Dark Lady had picked out for her, but surely a ninja wouldn't have any trouble walking that far on her tiptoes.

He and Kai were following along from the borderland and watching via a viewing portal. Kanna had the strut working as she approached the club, which was actually nicer than he expected, especially given the neighborhood. There was a line waiting to get in, with a pair of bouncers dressed in dark suits and built like brick walls deciding who entered and who didn't. Conryu had never been much for the club scene, but clearly plenty of people were. He counted forty people in the line outside.

"I never thought the grandmaster would be capable of such a transformation," Kai said.

"Pretty impressive, that's for sure. I knew she had the looks, but it's the attitude change that's really something. I'm going to need to take the Dark Lady on another date as a thank-you. Her coaching seems to have made all the difference. Look at that."

Kanna had strutted straight up to the door, ignoring the line completely. The bouncers took one look at her, lowered the velvet rope, and waved her in.

Conryu grinned and shifted their view to the inside of the club. The dance floor was filled with people bumping and grinding, drinks in their hands, and seeming to be having a grand time. In the center of the floor was the pit that gave the club its name. No one was fighting at the moment. Conryu had no idea if that was a nightly thing or if there was some sort of schedule.

He didn't care either. His attention had fallen on a massively built black man in a navy suit seated at a round booth on the back wall. Big Bob was here. Thank heaven for that. Given her earlier reactions, he doubted he could convince Kanna to do this two nights in a row. He doubted Jonny had that long either.

On the downside, he wasn't alone. Just as Conryu feared, there was one woman who crackled with a magical aura. She wore a red cocktail dress and had the curves of a stripper, but there was no mistaking her magical ability. The wizard worried him far more than the four men with bulging shoulder holsters behind Bob.

Kanna wove her way through the dancers, rebuffed the advances of several drunk men, and finally made it to the bar. One of the bartenders, a man Conryu guessed wasn't much older than he was, hurried over when he spotted Kanna.

She whispered something to him and kissed his cheek.

"Oh my," Kai muttered.

That summed up Conryu's feelings as well. The bartender staggered a couple steps, then sprinted over to Big Bob's table. He leaned closer and pointed back at Kanna. Bob took in an eyeful and nodded.

So far so good.

The bartender returned and paused to pour Kanna a drink. He also subtly slipped something into it, blocking the glass with his body so she wouldn't notice.

"Chosen," Kai said.

"I saw."

Conryu shifted their view and opened a micro portal just above the bar. When the bartender set the glass down, he shifted the portal directly below it and touched the glass. Light magic surged out, negating the poison and the alcohol.

Kanna took a drink as if she hadn't noticed anything, but there was no way she wouldn't have sensed the portal open from such a short range. Her acting skills really were impressive.

Once she'd drained the glass, Kanna stood and headed for Big Bob's table, strut turned to full power. A stride away, one of the goons as well as the wizard stepped forward. Kanna raised her arms and got patted down as well as checked for magic.

Conryu held his breath for that last one, but she passed without issue and soon found herself seated beside Big Bob.

"She made it past the first test," he muttered. "Now she just needs to get him alone."

There was a bit of chitchat as Kanna slid her hand further and further up Big Bob's leg. She had just about reached the good spot when Bob stood. He said something to his guards then he took Kanna by the hand. The pair left the club floor and took a set of steps to the second story. That turned out to be a very fancy apartment.

How convenient.

As soon as Bob turned away from the door, Conryu opened a portal, stepped out behind him, and touched the back of his head with the glowing tip of his staff. Bob went rigid as the light magic took control of his mind.

"Outstanding work, Kanna."

"Thank you, Chosen. Though I now feel an overwhelming need for a bath."

"Good idea. If anyone's listening in, they'll hear the water running and think things are getting started. Kai brought your uniform, so you can change when you're done."

"Now? I didn't really mean…"

"It's fine. Kai can keep watch while I'm digging around in his memories. As soon as I'm finished, we can get out of here."

Kanna took the ninja uniform from Kai and went to find the bathroom.

For his part, Conryu focused his will on Jonny and slipped into Bob's memories. The first one he found showed Jonny's arrival and the brutal beatdown of his first opponent. Bob had been well pleased with his new fighter. Conryu was surprised though—Jonny had never shown such a mean streak anytime they fought.

He shrugged and fast-forwarded through the next three fights, all wins for Jonny. After the last one, the view shifted to a man so thin he looked like a corpse in a suit. Since Jonny wasn't here, he had to be the subject of the discussion.

The memory slowed down to real time just as Bob said, "Yes, sir, Mr. Cadus. I've got a fighter that would be perfect for your tournament. He hasn't lost a fight yet."

"Has he killed anyone?" Cadus asked.

"We don't do death matches here. Too much of a pain in the ass."

"Not ideal, but I need one more to fill out the tournament roster. If he's not up to the challenge, he'll quickly be eliminated."

Bob shrugged. "No skin off my ass. You're paying me ten times what I'd make off him in a year anyway. Do whatever you want with him."

Cadus pointed and a goon with a briefcase appeared in the memory. He popped the latches, revealing stacks of hundred-dollar bills, at least a quarter million worth.

Bob grinned. "Pleasure doing business with you."

There was another brief memory of him telling Jonny about the tournament and how he'd make a fortune if he won.

And that was it. A quick search for anything more about Cadus came up empty. That appeared to be the first and only time Bob had spoken with the man. Maybe the Department had more info about him. Last but not least, he created a new memory of a night of wild sex with Kanna. It was a memory Bob would treasure forever, he felt certain.

Conryu opened his eyes and found Kanna, washed and dressed in her ninja outfit, standing beside Kai.

"Did you find what you were hoping for, Chosen?" Kai asked.

"I got a lead on who has Jonny now. I'll need to check with Maria for more details, assuming he has a record. What time is it anyway?"

"Just after midnight," Kanna said.

"Guess we'll have to wait until morning. Let's put our baby to bed and get out of here."

Conryu guided Bob to his bedroom and had him pause beside the bed. "Tear his clothes off. Think excited lover not honey badger."

Kai and Kanna exchanged looks. Moments later Bob's shirt, sans buttons, went flying one way, his pants another, and last his boxers. A final tap on the forehead with the staff sent him crashing to the bed, sound asleep.

It was time for them to leave. Much as he hated to wait, there was nothing more to be done until morning, and a few hours' sleep wouldn't do Conryu any harm.

10

The reference library at Kincade West had to be among the largest collections of magical knowledge in the world. There were thousands of books written in hundreds of languages, all helpfully translated into English. Even more important, as far as Malice was concerned, the researchers had compiled a complete, searchable registry. Now she just had to pray that the information she needed actually appeared in the books. Demon summoning wasn't her area of expertise.

"What should I do?" Miguel asked as she settled in front of the library computer.

Malice rejected the first rude comment that came to mind. She needed the fool happy and pliable. Riling him up would only make her job that much harder.

"You can keep watch. I don't believe the guards' patrol extends to the basement, but as with my access code, that may have changed. If anyone shows up, capture them and I'll erase their memories when I'm done."

"Is that something you can teach me?" Miguel asked. "It sounds useful."

"Certainly. The process is simple, but requires finesse. You basically take a tiny amount of dark magic and rot away the section of the target's brain that has recorded the memory. Light magic is much more effective for this sort of technique, but neither of us has access to that anymore, so we must make do."

Miguel nodded and went to stand by the door. Malice had discovered that if she took a few seconds to explain things to him, it did wonders to keep the complaints to a minimum. Of course, if he knew what she really planned, it wouldn't go over well. Lucky for her, his magical ability was so crude and limited that he couldn't even tell when someone lied right to his face.

Putting her master—Malice nearly laughed out loud at the idea of ever calling the boy master—out of her mind, she typed in a search for anything about demon summoning. That brought up a list of eight books, far fewer than she expected. Probably because there was no money in it.

She clicked on the first name and read the summary. It covered the basics of calling an imp and binding it as a familiar. Useless.

The next one looked equally basic, but the third at least had the word "advanced" in the title. Whoever summarized it must have been in a hurry as there were no useful details. She shrugged and jotted down its location. In the end she decided another three might be of some use and noted their locations as well.

Satisfied with her work, she switched the computer off.

"Did you find what you were looking for?" Miguel asked.

"Some of it. I won't know for sure until I read the books in more detail. According to the central computer, the source for the upgraded thralls I mentioned is unprotected, just as I hoped. That will be our temporary base for the time being."

She went to the shelf that held the first book on her list and Miguel followed along.

"Should we not get busy building a new temple to Baphomet? Once it's consecrated, our power will grow."

Malice was less eager to increase Baphomet's power on earth than a good demon should be. Fortunately, it wasn't that simple.

"Building a temple and sacrificing a wizard isn't enough now that the original temple has been purified and the demonic core destroyed. First, we need to create a new core, then summon a guardian demon to bind to it. Neither task is a simple one."

"Can you not serve as the guardian demon?"

"No. Guardian demons are a very specific thing; they're created by the demon lords to perform this exact task. Any old demon won't do."

"You're hardly any old demon."

Malice smiled and pulled the book she wanted off the shelf. Was he trying to flatter her? Hardly seemed likely. "You're right about that, but I'm still not a guardian demon. Be patient, I'm a demon and you're a hellpriest. Neither of us has to worry about growing old anymore. Better we do this right and not get caught."

As if on cue a shout came from the library doorway. "Hey! Both of you put your hands up. This is private property and you're trespassing."

A pair of security guards stood just inside the entrance, pistols leveled.

And things had been going so smoothly.

Before she could do anything, black vines shot out from every direction, wrapping the guards up like mummies. She gave a little nod to Miguel. He might not know much, but that little trick had happened so fast she hadn't even sensed him prepping the spell.

"Keep them bound while I collect the last of the books. I won't be long."

"The vines will hold them until I tell them to let go," Miguel said. "Will I get to see the memory-erasing spell?"

"We don't have much choice now." Malice hurried to collect the last three books then stuffed all four into a satchel she conjured out of summoned vines. It was crude, but would suffice for the moment.

"Why are you hurrying?"

"Because there are more guards and if these two called in intruders, we might have more company soon. I prefer not to have to waste my time erasing the memories of every guard in the building."

"We could always just kill them all and be done with it."

"No, that's a terrible idea. A talented dark magic user would be able to figure out how we killed them and Baphomet's magic is unique enough that word would certainly get back to *him*. And once it did, he'll never stop looking for us."

Miguel shuddered. "Understood. Let's get going."

Malice strode over to the guards and summoned a tiny spark of dark magic. Focusing on their minds, she erased the most recent five minutes of their memories. Both of them blacked out during the process, which suited her fine. The subtle damage to their brains would be nearly invisible to even the most skilled wizard. An autopsy would be hard-pressed to reveal the damage for what it really was. A doctor was apt to mistake the tiny wounds as damage from a mini stroke.

"Done. What's the range of your transportation spell?"

"That was amazing," Miguel said. "I never imagined anyone could use such a tiny amount of magic."

"It just takes practice. The spell?"

"Right. As far as I know, I can go anywhere I can picture as long as there are plants present."

"Perfect."

Malice projected the destination she wanted into his mind and a moment later the earth swallowed them up.

11

I t was incredibly difficult to tell the time when you were underground. At least Jonny assumed the arena was underground. Why else would there be no windows? And he still had no idea where he'd ended up. Despite devoting a great deal of his time to thinking about his situation, he'd come up with no reasonable answers. In the end he'd shrugged and gone to sleep.

Now, his body argued morning had arrived. His time in the military had seen him up and moving by five every day and even though he'd only been in the army for a couple years, he still found he woke up at the same time despite his best efforts to sleep in.

With nothing better to do, he rolled out of bed, hit the head, and ambled down the hall to the cafeteria. The room was dark and silent, more's the pity. Just out of curiosity, he made his way to the end of the hall and up into the arena. The seats were empty and the space silent. Not a great surprise assuming he'd guessed right about the hour.

Were the big shots around here somewhere? He assumed the suits lived elsewhere, but Loong should be on the premises. No way would they leave so many antisocial people totally on their own.

He strode out onto the sand, getting a feel for it, how his footing would be, and generally doing what little he could to prepare. It was weird being in the empty arena. It felt both new and old all at once, like a relic out of time that hadn't aged in centuries.

For all he knew, this might be some Roman arena that they fixed up. At the very least the odds of his backup finding him here seemed remote. And that was a serious problem since Jonny had seen no signs of an actual exit.

Most likely only the winner would see daylight again. Everyone else would be carried out on a stretcher with a white cloth covering their body.

Jonny put the unsettling thought out of his mind and did a little shadow boxing. The sand wasn't as firm as he'd like and he found his punches and kicks had a fraction less power than usual. Against an opponent like Lala, that might be enough of a difference to cost him dearly. Of course, his murderous new friend would have the same problem, so maybe it would all even out.

A faint smile tugged at his lips. It might even out if Lala wasn't twice his size.

Slow clapping filled the space and he turned to find one of the suits emerging from an arched entryway. It was the healthy-looking one, Mr. Asterion. His flunkies were absent today, for the moment at least.

"I'm impressed to see you making such careful preparations," Asterion said. "Given your failure to kill a single adversary in your earlier matches, I had little hope that you'd amount to anything save a warmup for Lala. Perhaps I judged you too quickly."

Jonny's body had tensed up as Asterion approached and he tried to relax. Something about the man's presence put him more on guard than even Loong's did. He might be well put together, but there was no way a simple businessman should put Jonny so on edge.

"Like I told Lala yesterday, I wasn't required to kill to win my fights, so I didn't. Don't mistake my lack of eagerness for unwillingness to do whatever it takes to survive."

"A splendid attitude. That will, that desire to survive no matter what, is what I love about fighters. Do you think it's odd for someone like me to be hanging around a place like this, not to mention putting up the huge prize that the winner will claim?"

Jonny shrugged. "I don't know you or anything about you. From your looks and that huge chest of gold, I figure you're rich. Rich people do all sorts of weird shit. This is hardly the farthest-out-there thing I've heard of. If hanging out with fighters and watching them beat the hell out of each other is your jam, far be it from me to question."

Asterion smiled, his teeth looking more gold than white. Was he wearing a gold-plated grill? Jonny had this dude pegged as a weirdo, but he was getting weirder by the second.

"Coming into this," Asterion said. "I marked Lala as my favorite, but having met you, I now find that I hope you survive and claim the final prize."

"You and me both."

"I'll let you return to your training. Best of luck, Jonny Salazar."

Jonny went cold and watched Asterion's back as he strode away. How could he know Jonny's last name? He'd gone undercover with an alias, Jonny Salamanca. Only his backup and his bosses should know who he really was. Certainly not some businessman from who the hell knew where.

He'd thought he was in the shit up to his chin, but now he was wondering if even his eyeballs were showing.

Jonny enjoyed a hot breakfast with Lala, who was happy to keep up the chatter from the previous day. He found it astonishing, despite what he'd learned about Lala yesterday, that the man could just chat casually with someone he was going to try and kill in a few hours. Of course, Jonny was doing pretty much the same thing, so what did that say about him?

When everyone had finished eating and the conversations were getting louder, Loong entered the cafeteria. A hush fell over the room. They all had a pretty good idea what the man's arrival meant.

"Alright, it's that time. Hardgrave and Santana, you're up first. Anyone wants to watch, there's a special box reserved for the fighters. Don't talk to the patrons and keep your comments to a minimum. The people are here to watch the fight, not listen to you lot jabber."

"His personality hasn't improved overnight," Lala murmured as they stood to follow the others out.

Jonny quirked an eyebrow. "Did you think it might?"

"A man can hope."

"Sure he can. There's a saying in the Alliance, though I have no idea if there's something similar in Turkey. It goes, hope in one hand, shit in the other, and see which one fills up first."

"No, I've never heard such a disgusting sentiment before. Though I do take your meaning. Better not to hope but to take matters into your own hands. A fine sentiment for a fighter."

Jonny didn't know how fine it was. Taking matters into his own hands wasn't going to amount to much. Hoping Conryu somehow found him and came to the rescue seemed far likelier to do him good.

They trooped into the arena and unlike during Jonny's early morning visit, the stands were packed with people. Cheers went up as the fighters entered and a few waved at the crowd like this was just an MMA event. Jonny gave the patrons a close look and frowned. It had to be his imagination, but some of them looked like duplicates. One set of twins he could imagine, but he counted four identical faces in just the first section of seats they passed.

The first two fighters broke off and headed for the center of the ring. Loong stayed with the main group until they reached a section of seats divided from the rest of the arena by stone partitions. Jonny sat beside the partition with Lala on his left.

When everyone had settled in, Loong left them to their own devices with only a hard glare to remind them to behave. Their keeper, at least that's how Jonny had come to think of the man, strode across the sand and stopped between the fighters.

Hardgrave and Santana looked like an even match to Jonny. Similar height and build, same hard eyes that said they wouldn't give two seconds' thought to killing someone. Jonny hoped his eyes never looked like that and he really hoped Conryu's never did. If there was one thing the world should fear, it was his friend losing his distaste for killing.

"What do you think?" Jonny asked.

"Hard to say having never seen either fight." Lala twirled his mustache around his finger. "They'll probably open cautiously, feel each other out. First mistake ends it."

"Ladies and gentlemen!" Loong's voice thundered out at far greater volume than should've been possible. "Welcome to the first match of the day. You have five minutes to place your bets using the terminals provided. When that time is up, the match will begin. There are no rules. This is pure survival of the fittest. Wizards, if you will join me on the sand. The betting period begins now."

Loong fell silent and a moment later two women—young, hot women at that—emerged from the tunnel opposite where the fighters had come from. They wore very little: bikini tops and short skirts slit up to the waist. Both of them would've looked right at home on Miami Beach.

"They're like ring girls," one of the fighters further down the line muttered.

That's exactly what they were, or so Jonny thought until they broke apart and each went to a different fighter. The girl in the red top went to Hardgrave. He grinned at her, but the woman remained stone-faced. She raised her hands and red flames laced with streaks of black twisted around Hardgrave's arms, legs, and chest.

"What the hell?" Hardgrave staggered a step back, seeming surprised despite knowing that magic would be involved in the fights.

The wizard ignored him, her flat expression never wavering. It wasn't natural, though Jonny didn't know what it was.

When the woman in the white top finished, Santana's body was surrounded in crackling, crimson lightning.

That wasn't right either. Jonny had learned a little about magic during basic training, then a good deal more when he transferred to the Department of Infernal Investigation. He'd assumed based on the color of their clothes that the first girl was fire aligned and the second light aligned. The flames certainly argued for the first, but light magic lightning wasn't that color. It should be white or slightly golden. But crimson? No, something weird was going on here.

He lifted his gaze and scanned the crowd. Soon enough he spotted a box separate from the rest of the arena seats. He flinched when he realized Asterion was staring right at him. Jonny was too far away to see the man's expression, but he suspected it was a grin.

What was he playing at? If he knew who Jonny really was, he had to know why he was here. Assuming that, why hadn't he just ended the charade at once? So many things didn't add up and Jonny wanted to know why even as he feared to find out.

"Time's up!" Loong's voice jolted him out of his thoughts. "Betting is closed. Fighters, you can use your power however you think best. But remember it's not limitless. Once you're out, you're out. Ready? Fight!"

Loong sprinted for the arched exit where he stood safely out of the way.

Fire and lightning flashed and crashed as the fighters let loose with everything they had. At least it looked to Jonny like they were. Neither fought with any particular skill or control. Though to be fair, he doubted either man had ever wielded magic before.

"I don't like this," Lala said. "It was supposed to be a contest between warriors, not a light show."

"Not a fan of magic?"

Lala shrugged. "It's not a thing for men to worry about. Muscle and bone and will should settle things, not tricks."

Jonny nodded, but didn't reply. Personally, he wouldn't mind a few tricks if he was fighting Lala. He'd seen a bit of how Conryu used magic and had a few ideas that might work to his advantage, assuming he got earth magic. It was a one-in-six shot, but he would keep his fingers crossed.

Down on the sand, the fighters had used up their tricks and were now pummeling each other the old-fashioned way. They exchanged a few blows until a right cross from Santana sent Hardgrave to his knees.

Santana pounced, wrapping his arm around Hardgrave's neck and pulling back until an audible crunch filled the air. Santana stood and threw his hands in the air as the crowd cheered. In the end, the magic hadn't really done anything to affect the outcome, but it had been an impressive show.

"They should just skip the magic," Lala said as Loong led Santana back to the waiting area where Jonny assumed the hot light aligned wizard was waiting to ease his pain. "None of us know how to use it anyway."

Lala had a point. There was only one man that knew how to wield magic and he was far from here, much to Jonny's disappointment. Were they adding it purely for dramatic effect? He could hardly find fault with their reasoning given the many oohs and ahhs from the crowd as the magic roared around.

Jonny shrugged. It was what it was. As fighters, it was their job to adapt to the circumstances, not complain about them.

When the body had been carried off on a stretcher by a pair of nervous-looking men, Loong returned and called out the next pair of names. They got their magic and went at it. The results weren't all that different from the first match. Lots of flash and thunder that ended with a bareknuckle brawl and a fresh corpse.

The pattern continued until Jonny and Lala were called to the sand. He swallowed the lump in his throat and stood.

Lala clapped him on the back. "I hope you will give me a good fight, my friend."

He sounded like he meant it. Jonny just hoped he could figure out some way for both of them to get out of this alive.

12

K elsie Kincade sat in her mother's office in Kincade Manor and stared at the little counter on her computer screen. One hundred and fifty-seven emails needed her attention and the number kept growing every second. In fact, despite her diligent efforts, she'd never gotten the number down to zero for even a moment. Just when she thought she'd finished, another one showed up. Emails were like cockroaches; no matter how many you killed there was always one more hiding in a dark corner.

She sighed and rubbed the bridge of her nose. Things were actually better now than when she first took over. It turned out that several of the former White Witches that she'd let move into an empty apartment building the company owned had experience with paperwork and knew how to function in a large organization. As soon as Kelsie heard that, she hired the women on the spot as her personal assistants. They all worked at the Kincade building downtown, but Kelsie preferred to work from home. She had an office of course, on the top floor with a gorgeous view of Central.

One day at headquarters had convinced her of the joys of

telecommuting. At least here she didn't have people knocking on her door with problems. Instead she got emails.

The phone rang and she nearly jumped out of her chair. Not many people had the number for the office phone and none of the people that did would use it unless there was a major problem. The sort of problem Kelsie really didn't want to deal with.

On the third ring she snatched up the handset. "This is Kelsie."

"My name is Artyom Gladyr, ma'am, chief of security for Kincade Industries."

Kelsie frowned. She didn't recognize the name. Not terribly surprising given the size of the business, but it seemed like she'd have met the chief of security.

"I don't believe we've been properly introduced, Chief Gladyr. How can I help you today?"

"I apologize for not coming to see you in person, ma'am, but I've been on a tour, inspecting all of Kincade Industries' facilities. Your mother gave the order right after assuming full control of the business. Since there was no company-wide meeting, I just kept doing what I was doing. As for how you can help, I'm not sure if you can. There was a break-in last night at Kincade West. The news just reached me, so I don't have all the details, but it seemed like the sort of thing you'd want to know about. The strange thing is, whoever broke in tried to use your grandmother's access code."

Kelsie's heart skipped a beat. "Whatever you're doing, Chief, stop at once and focus on this break-in. I want all the details as soon as possible. Draw on whatever resources you need. If anyone gives you any shit, tell them to call me and I'll help them find new employment. This is your top priority and I expect daily updates."

"Understood, ma'am. I'm on the West Coast now and should have at least a basic update by noon. I just wanted to confirm— your friend the male wizard didn't do this, right?"

"No. If Conryu needed something he'd ask me. Plus I'm sure Grandmother would never share her access code with him."

"That's what I figured, but better to ask than to step in something I shouldn't. If there's nothing else, I'll get moving."

"There is one more thing. You report only to me about this matter. A break-in so soon after I take over isn't a good look and I'd prefer word not get around."

"Yes, ma'am. I'll be in touch this afternoon."

He disconnected and Kelsie returned the handset to its cradle. Her heart had slowed to a more normal rhythm, but hearing her grandmother's code had been used sent a shock through her. Malice was dead, burned to nothing by Conryu's magic, but even so she still terrified Kelsie in a way no one else could.

She snapped her fingers. Despite her confidence, she didn't actually know for sure that Conryu hadn't broken in to the campus. He might have been in a hurry and not wanted to bother her. Better to call and make sure. It wasn't that she wanted to hear his reassuring voice.

Certainly not.

Pulling out her cell, she opened her contact list and tapped his name. After two rings he said, "Hey, Kelsie. What's up?"

"There's been a bit of a situation at Kincade West and I wanted to make sure it wasn't you." She gave him the few details she knew.

"I haven't left Central in a day and a half. Jonny's in a mess and I'm trying to dig him out. Who could be using Malice's code?"

"I don't know. Given Grandmother's personality, I doubt she'd share it with anyone. All I can think is that someone got into her papers and found it. Our chief of security is looking into it, so hopefully he can sort things out quickly."

"Quick is always good." She could hear the grin in his voice. "Whatever happens, keep me informed. If you need help, shout. I'm never more than a hell portal away."

"I wouldn't want to bother you with my family business's problems."

"You know better than that and I never want you to use the word bother in the context of you calling me. Okay?"

She nearly cried, but kept her voice steady. "Okay. Thank you."

"You bet. I gotta go. Maria and I are about to talk with her father. Take care."

He hung up and she stared at her phone and sighed. Would Kelsie ever reach a point in her life where she didn't need Conryu to either reassure her or rescue her? She smiled to herself. More importantly, did she really want to get to that point?

If Kelsie was being completely honest with herself, the answer was no.

———

Conryu gave a little shake of his head and pocketed his phone. He didn't really think Kelsie's problem would end up in his lap, though of course if she needed him, Conryu would do everything possible to help. Hearing Malice's name after killing her not that long ago sent a chill up his spine. She had to have been the evilest old woman on the planet. If anyone deserved to get purified by white flames, it was her.

"What sort of trouble is she in now?" Maria asked.

The two of them were standing in the waiting room outside Maria's father's office. Unlike usual, his secretary hadn't just waved them in. It seemed he was on the phone with someone and needed a minute to finish up. Conryu didn't particularly care, but he did hope it didn't take too long since he was eager to learn more about Cadus and hopefully get a lead on Jonny.

"Too soon to say." Conryu shared the gist of the conversation. "Hopefully it's just corporate espionage and her security guy can handle it."

"And if it's not?" Maria asked.

"You know what happens if it's not. I won't let her get herself killed. Kelsie's a sweetheart and I worry that she's not cutthroat enough for the path she's chosen. But it's her path to walk, all I can do is support her."

The intercom buzzed and Mr. Kane's slightly staticky voice said, "Send them in."

Amy waved them on and Maria took the lead.

"Any idea what he wants to talk about?" Conryu asked.

"You know what I know." She knocked once then pushed the door open.

Mr. Kane stood up behind his slightly messy desk when they entered, hugged Maria, and shook Conryu's hand. "Thanks for taking the time. I know you're busy, but I just received some disturbing news."

"Seems to be a lot of that going around," Conryu said. "Lay it on me."

"Do you remember the wannabe druids out in Washington?"

Conryu nodded. "Sure. You said the Seattle office checked them out and everything was good."

"That's what they told me. However, a civilian wizard in the area detected a powerful burst of dark magic and when the team was dispatched to take a second look, they found the buildings ruined and no sign of the people. A lingering aura of dark magic remained."

How come every time he trusted other people to handle things, everything went to shit?

"Just dark magic? Nothing else mixed in that might suggest a hellpriest was involved?"

"Not according to the report. But several days had passed before the team arrived. When I spoke to Angeline she indicated that the leftover magic could have broken down considerably in that time."

"That terrifying woman is correct," Prime said. "The fact that any magic is detectable indicates that a powerful ritual was performed."

"That was the on-site assessment as well. Unfortunately, they couldn't figure out exactly what the magic's purpose was."

"I'm sure its purpose will become clear when it bites us in the ass. I appreciate the update, but I really need to do some research. I've got a line on a guy I think might know where Jonny is, but all I know about him is a name and what he looks like."

"Least I can do is run the search for you," Mr. Kane said. "Give me what you have."

"His name is Cadus and he looks like a refugee from the zombie apocalypse: tall, gaunt, pale." Conryu stopped talking when he noticed Mr. Kane wasn't typing what he said. "What's wrong?"

"His name popped up as soon as I entered it. Nicolai Cadus, suspected in more crimes than I care to name, no arrests. Jonny's team saw him make contact with Big Bob and managed to get a couple pictures to confirm."

Conryu looked from Maria to her dad. "You didn't think to mention this in the briefing?"

Mr. Kane winced. "It's complicated. There's an open case against him being investigated by a different department. They requested we keep our distance so he didn't get spooked."

Conryu stood. "You realize this is why I hate working with the government."

"I know, son, I know. Since it's integral to our investigation and we have an undercover agent in danger, they can't complain too loudly if we poke our noses in a little deeper." Mr. Kane clicked his mouse and the printer on the corner of his desk whirred to life, spitting out a single sheet of paper. He handed it to Conryu. "Here you go. Contact information, known associates, everything we've got."

"Thanks. I need to move. If anything comes of those other matters, let me know. If I learn anything about Jonny, I'll be in touch." He kissed Maria on the cheek and hurried out the door.

As soon as he reached the hall, Conryu opened a hell portal and stepped through.

"I feel your anger, Chosen," Kai said. "What do you wish me to do?"

He took a deep, steadying breath. "About Mr. Kane and his bureaucratic bullshit, nothing. But you could take a quick trip to check in with Kelsie's guards and make sure they're extra alert. If something's going on that has anything to do with Malice, I want no screwups. Don't worry, I'll wait for you to get back."

She bowed and flew off toward, he assumed, Kincade Manor.

"What will you do should the people from this other department attempt to stop you from contacting Cadus?" Prime asked.

"I'll calmly explain the situation like a reasonable person. And if that doesn't work I'll send them through a portal to France."

"Why France?" Prime asked.

"Why not France? As long as it's at least five time zones away, I don't care where they end up. Min."

An instant later the ninja assigned to keep an eye on Mr. Kane appeared. "Yes, Chosen?"

"Did you know about Cadus?"

She shook her head. "As I said, I can only hear one side of the conversations. If the name was mentioned, it was by the person Mr. Kane spoke to."

Conryu's frown deepened. "That might not be good enough if he's keeping secrets. I mean, I knew he was keeping secrets, but I'm talking about important stuff. Prime, is there some magic that will let the lookouts listen in on conversations?"

"No, Master. The Daughters, for all their many talents, aren't skilled enough at pure casting to use the necessary spells. However, there are demons that have acute-enough hearing to listen in."

He turned to Min. "You don't have any issues working with a demon, do you?"

"Not if you wish me to."

"Great. I'll see about summoning and binding whatever critter Prime thinks can do the job. You'll be specified as its master."

She bowed. "As you wish, Chosen. And my apologies for being unable to complete your task on my own."

"We've all got our limitations. Don't give it a second thought."

He spotted Kai returning. Good, he'd wasted enough time this morning. Hopefully summoning the demon wouldn't take long.

It was time to find Jonny and bring him home safe.

13

Conryu whistled and stared up at the high-rise across the street from where he'd appeared. Thirty stories of gleaming steel and glass, the building was listed as belonging to Cadus and serving as both his home and place of business. His legitimate business, that was, some sort of import-export brokerage. The top floor was an apartment and that's where Conryu planned to get started.

Kai appeared beside him and bowed. "I have searched the perimeter as you requested. There are no wards that I can sense and no sign of guards."

"Okay, that's both convenient and weird. If this guy's such a big shot, there should at a minimum be men in too-tight suits with machine guns around to dissuade door-to-door salesmen. Something's up."

Conryu opened a hell portal behind him out of sight and stepped back into it. An extremely short trip brought him to the hall outside Cadus's apartment. Through a viewing portal, he confirmed everything Kai said.

The truth was, he could have just done this in the first place, but sending Kai in for a little scouting now and then made her feel like she was doing her job properly and hopefully would eliminate any more foolishness like her occasional desire to put herself in unnecessary danger.

A minor effort of will shifted them to the inside of the apartment. He grimaced. There were bodies everywhere, along with pools of dried blood. It looked like the floor of a slaughterhouse.

"Someone made a mess," Conryu said. "Nasty as it is, we need to take a closer look. Kai, check the rest of the apartment please."

He opened a portal well away from the carnage and stepped out. Picking his way around the various spatters, Conryu moved to the nearest body. Even with half its face missing, he was certain it wasn't Cadus. Inside what was once a blue suit jacket and now resembled a bum's blanket, he found a wallet.

"Well, shit." There was a government ID inside. Department of Major Crimes, Special Agent Danforth. "Agent Danforth, it seems you had a bad day. Prime, can you tell how long ago this happened?"

"How precise do you need me to be?" Prime asked.

"Jonny disappeared two days ago. Before or after that is sufficient."

"After," Prime said without hesitation. "I'd say less than a day ago. And they weren't shot to death or killed with magic."

"I noticed. Looks like they were torn apart by something with claws. What do you want to bet a demon was involved?"

"Nothing, given my confidence that you're correct. I sense no dark magic lingering, so whatever did this is certainly gone."

Kai appeared beside him. "No one else is present, Chosen, and I found no more bodies."

"The lack of more bodies is certainly a good thing. The lack of Cadus to interrogate is a problem. Do me a favor and see if this building has a security room. I want to know who has visited this apartment over the past week or so."

Kai vanished again and he got back to his grim task. It took only a few minutes and luckily a bit of magic kept the blood from sticking to him. Still, when this was over, he was going to need a shower.

All the bodies belonged to the same department. Something must have happened to convince them to raid the apartment. Maybe Mr. Kane could find out for him.

He lined up the IDs and snapped a picture with his phone. He texted the attachment, along with a short note, to Maria. Let her deal with her father. He had a few more stops to make.

Kai returned and said, "I found the security room, but there were two guards on duty. No wards were visible."

"Great, thanks. Let's go see what we can see."

He portaled them to the security room and as soon as they appeared Conryu paralyzed the guards so they couldn't sound the alarm. Dealing with the guards was easy, but figuring out the bank of sixteen monitors, the server racks, and computer controls was another matter. While he was far from a technophobe, this level of tech was beyond him. Happily, he knew exactly the right person to help him.

He conjured a sound barrier around the room and tapped a number on his phone. Three rings later his mother said, "Hi sweetie, what's up?"

"I need a hand with some technology. Are you free?"

"Sure, I'm not in the middle of anything right now. What sort of technology?"

"A security system. I need to see everyone that came and went from a particular location for the past week or so. Is that something you know how to do?"

"Nothing to it." He could almost hear her frown. "Where are you exactly?"

He told her. "I'll pick you up in a sec."

Conryu hung up before she could lecture him about breaking the law. He'd hear it in person soon enough. "Keep an eye on things here, Kai. I won't be long."

"Yes, Chosen." She bowed and faded into the borderland.

Since his mother couldn't safely travel through Hell, Conryu opened the library. He willed it to her workshop at the Department and opened the door.

When he stepped out, a voice from behind him said, "That was fast."

He turned and smiled at his mother. She had on her work coveralls, but didn't have any grease on her face yet and her hair was still in a neat ponytail. He must have caught her before she got started for the day. It had been far too long since he went to visit her. Having to save the world on a regular basis, while a fact, seemed like a lame excuse.

He hugged her. "Fast is my middle name. Come on, I'm sure the two guards I paralyzed are eager for us to finish our business and set them free."

He helped her into the library and closed the door.

"I know you've got important things to do," she said. "But aren't you playing a little too fast and loose with the law?"

"Maybe, but given the alternatives I'll take my chances. Don't worry, the guards won't even see you or know you're there."

An instant later they were stepping back down out of the library into the security station. Kai appeared a moment later and bowed to them both. "Nothing happened while you were gone, Chosen."

"Thanks, Kai. Mom, I need to see everyone that went into the apartment on the top floor. How can I help?"

She looked from one unmoving guard to the other. "I just need a place to sit."

That was easy. A thought and gesture brought one of the guards to his feet before he shuffled to one side, zombielike. The other one never even flinched as his mother sat beside him and started typing.

All but one of the screens went blank and time seemed to fast-forward. He watched the clock on the screen spin by at about an hour every ten seconds. Finally, someone appeared. The image froze and zoomed in. Four days ago, a man in a dark suit arrived. Conryu could tell little about him from the black-and-white image beyond his slightly dark complexion and muscular build. He certainly didn't match the appearance of Cadus's closest known associate, an obese man named Bund.

"Okay, Mom."

The image started moving again. Twelve hours passed then twenty-four. Still no sign that Cadus or the stranger had come back out. Sixteen hours ago a group of five men strode down the hall. One knocked but got no response. Four drew their weapons while the fifth knelt to open the lock. They all rushed in and then there was nothing.

"That's it," his mother said.

"Thanks, Mom, that was a big help. I'll run you back now."

"What did all that mean and what happened in that apartment?" she asked.

"I'm not completely sure what it meant and if I tell you what happened in the apartment, you're unlikely to be able to sleep tonight. It was not pretty."

"Tell me. I'm your mother and I need to know what you're dealing with day in and day out."

He looked into her eyes and saw no sign that she'd relent. "If you're sure."

Conryu told her everything they found with only mild editing. "We're pretty certain they ran into a demon. How the demon got there is another matter, one of the ones I'm not sure about. Cadus, the guy I wanted to talk to, never came out, which means someone magicked him out, probably the first guy we saw go in. I know he got out at some point because he talked to Big Bob after the stranger came to visit him. Worst of all, Jonny's in the middle of all this and I'm not certain where he is."

She wrapped her arms around him. "This is too much for just you... and Kai of course."

"I won't argue," Conryu said. "But this is the way it has to be if we want to keep the loss of innocent lives to a minimum. I've spoken to the powers that be about the alternatives, and none of them are good."

She stepped back and shook her head. "I don't have to like it. And you're too thin. You should be eating more."

"I'll do my best, Mom. Let's get you back."

A quick trip via the library and they were back in her workshop. Conryu dropped his mother off after a final hug and worried look and returned to the security room. All that remained was to erase the last half hour or so of the guards' memories.

As he worked Kai asked, "What now, Chosen?"

"Now we see if Mr. Bund is in a chatty mood or if he's been disappeared as well. If he has, the only option left is a return to Fists of Steel and forcing our way past the barrier you found. I really hope I'm wrong, but I've got a strong feeling that if we do that, Jonny will be in even worse trouble than he is now."

14

Jonny stood facing Lala with about ten feet of sand separating them. Lala was grinning like this was all a game. Through all the craziness since they arrived, the one thing that hadn't changed was that smile. Fighting with his life on the line seemed to bring Lala genuine pleasure.

How did the saying go, it took all kinds to make a world?

The wizards in their skimpy ring-girl outfits emerged from the arched tunnel, one in white and the other in brown. The one in brown, the earth magic wizard, walked up to Jonny. How could he have gotten so lucky? His one idea for how to use the magic demanded he have access to earth magic and here she was to grant his wish. If it had been possible, Jonny would've gone out this second to buy a lottery ticket.

He glanced up at the VIP box and gulped. Asterion was staring right back at him. Jonny would've bet his nonexistent life savings that somehow the boss man had arranged for Jonny to get exactly the power he wanted. How Asterion knew what Jonny wanted, along with how he knew his name, remained a mystery.

The wizard raised her hands and looked at him with a blank, glassy expression. Her dead gaze never wavered as she raised her hands and power flowed into Jonny. As it did, he became acutely aware of the sand beneath his feet and how the power might let him control it.

His wizard backed away and he got a look at Lala, who had lightning sparking around his clenched fists. His attacks would be far faster than Jonny's, but as Lala said, he didn't know anything about using magic. Hopefully that meant his attacks would be clumsy and awkward.

When the women were safely out of the way Loong said, "Ready? Fight!"

Jonny dove right an instant ahead of a lightning bolt.

He rolled to his feet and immediately sprang in another direction.

Lightning flashed all around him, as clumsy as he'd hoped but more lethal than he feared.

Constant movement and a hastily conjured wall of sand kept Jonny alive as Lala lashed out with one blast after another.

The crowd roared, seeming louder now than ever.

Jonny dove and rolled one more time before he realized that no more lightning was incoming. When he came to his feet, Lala's fist was closing in fast.

Jonny turned away, but still took a glancing blow.

The room spun, but no shock ran through him. Lala had to be out of power.

Magical power at least.

The right heel that whizzed past Jonny's head made it clear that he still had plenty of the old-fashioned kind of power left.

Jonny needed space and a second to concentrate.

A wave of his hand sent a spray of sand into Lala's face, staggering him back a step.

Now, what did Conryu call the spell? Stone Skin, right.

Focus. Imagine your skin becoming hard as granite.

The hair on Jonny's arms stood up. That had to be a good sign, didn't it?

His answer came a moment later when Lala's fist crashed into his face and he felt nothing more than a light pressure.

Lala hopped back, cradling his right hand. "Dirty fighting, Jonny."

"And what were all those lightning bolts you threw at me? It's not my fault you missed."

Jonny charged, rock-hard fists leading.

Lala dodged his first swing, but the second took him in the ribs. Something gave when the blow landed, drawing a grunt from Lala.

A quick kick to the knee crumpled Lala's right leg.

Finally a hard right hook sent him to the sand, out cold.

Jonny raised his hands, but the crowd stayed silent.

Loong emerged from the tunnel, his craggy face set in a particularly deep scowl. "He's still alive. The fight's not over until one of you is dead."

"He's down and out. Broken ribs, busted knee, and at least a concussion. I'm not going to murder a helpless man in cold blood. Disqualify us both if you have to, I don't care."

Loong reached behind his back, pulled out a pistol, and pointed it at the back of Lala's head. "If you're too squeamish, I'll end it for you."

Magic surged at Jonny's command and when Loong fired, the bullet bounced off Lala's now-rock-hard skin.

"Miserable punk!" Loong leveled the gun at Jonny. "I'll take care of you both."

"That's quite enough." Both of their gazes shifted to Asterion, who had emerged from another tunnel. "Given that he was the only one to use the magic in a remotely creative way, it would be a waste to kill Jonny. And as the loser, Lala's life is utterly irrelevant. Return to the dorm and rest, the next round begins in an hour."

With that pronouncement, Asterion turned on his heel and marched back out.

"Lucky you're the boss's new favorite." Loong holstered his pistol. "We'll see if your luck holds next round."

With a wave of his hand Loong brought the nervous stretcher-bearers running. Jonny helped them load Lala and followed them back to the dorm. Though Jonny hadn't taken enough damage to say so, he hoped Asterion would be generous and let the light magic user repair the worst of Lala's injuries. The blows to his head and his body might have done some serious internal damage.

The surviving fighters all stared when Jonny entered. None spoke, but he had little trouble imagining some of the thoughts going through their heads. Some worried about his skill using the magic. Others probably thought he was weak for sparing Lala. His next opponent—Jonny would have to check the brackets to see who it was—might even be relieved that he was fighting someone reluctant to kill.

Jonny didn't care what any of them thought as long as they left him and Lala alone. The bearers transferred Lala to an empty cot and hurried out. The light magic wizard brushed past them as she entered. Jonny blew out a sigh of relief.

"Start with Lala. He's in way worse shape than me."

The woman shook her head and stopped beside Jonny. "He lost. Whether he lives or dies is of no concern to the master."

The pain from Lala's punch quickly faded as warmth flooded into him. It was different from when Conryu healed him, but plenty welcome all the same. In seconds he felt in perfect shape.

She lowered her hands and took a step towards the door.

Jonny grabbed her wrist. "Can't you do anything for him?"

She jerked free with more strength than her slender arm should possess. "I received no orders from the master. Without those, I will do nothing."

Jonny shook his head as she walked out. What the hell was that about "the master"? No one called their employer master in this day and age. It was weird, just like pretty much everything about this place. It felt like he'd fallen into a time warp that led to a thousand years in the past.

Lala groaned and opened his eyes. Both of them were red where the capillaries had burst. Not a great sign that he'd come through without internal injuries.

"Why am I still alive?" Lala asked.

"Because I decided I didn't need to kill you to win. How are you? Sorry, stupid question. Can I get you anything?"

"I need nothing at the moment." Lala scrubbed his hand across his face. "You should have killed me. Now your next opponent will think you're weak."

"Did you think I was weak?" Jonny asked.

"Somewhat, yes."

"See how that worked out for you. It'll work out the same for the next guy, who doesn't happen to be my friend. I promise I'll do my best to get us both out of here alive."

Jonny just hoped he'd be able to keep that promise.

15

A rtyom Gladyr, chief of security for Kincade Industries, climbed out of his company car in front of Kincade West's main building. The glass-and-steel building shone bright in the midday sun, nearly so bright he couldn't look at it. A knot of six security guards stood near the entrance, two of them holding their heads and looking like they'd just gotten back from a weeklong bender. He knew only the vaguest details about the incident, but agreed wholeheartedly with Ms. Kincade's order to make the investigation a top priority.

He also knew very little about the young lady that had just assumed control of the most powerful company on the planet, but if she'd survived twenty-plus years in that family, she had to be tough. She'd need to be if she wanted to make it as CEO.

Putting his new employer out of his mind, Artyom straightened his tie and smoothed his dark suit jacket. He strode over and the guards, the healthy ones at least, came immediately to attention. Since most of them were ex-military this wasn't a surprise. Artyom had been a major when he took early retirement.

"Where's the shift commander?" Artyom asked.

94

An older man in his midforties took a step forward. "Here sir, Blythe."

Blythe didn't salute, but it was clear he wanted to. His right hand even flinched up a fraction.

"What happened here, Blythe?"

"Two unknown parties entered the main building and accessed the central computer as well as the library. We found four books missing. As best we can tell, two guards stumbled across them and had their memories erased."

"The subjects of the missing books?" Artyom asked.

Blythe stared. "I don't know, sir. I didn't think to check. They were in the dark magic section, beyond that I couldn't say."

Artyom nodded, disappointed but not surprised. They were guards not investigators, after all. "I'll need to check both computers they accessed as well as any footage."

"Not a problem, sir. The footage is cued up in the central computer room and the library is at your disposal. We've kept everyone out of the library and only one tech has come and gone from the computer room. Sir, Vice President Kincade has been breathing down my neck, demanding to know when everyone can get back to work. What should I tell him?"

"Nothing. If he contacts you again, tell him we're acting on the CEO's orders and to call his niece if he had further questions. My best advice is for everyone that works in the main building to go home for the day. Now, show me to the central computer room."

The pair strode past the guards and into the building. Artyom hadn't been here in years, but it looked like everything remained in the same place. When they reached the door to the computer room he found the access panel outside still spitting sparks.

"Best get the power shut off to that panel. We don't need a fire on top of all our other problems."

"Yes, sir," Blythe said. "If you're all set, I'll take care of that right now."

"That's fine. I'm familiar with the computer system."

Artyom strode into the room and settled in a nice, soft office chair in front of the central monitor. A frozen image filled the screen. It showed two figures in masks and dressed in dark robes standing outside the main gate.

He pushed play and watched as the shorter figure punched something into the control panel, probably Malice's access code, and when that failed a tiny streak of darkness shot out and the gate slid partway open.

Given the height and magic, the shorter one was certainly a woman. The pair ran across the driveway and entered the main building the same way they did the front gate. From there they came here and the recording stopped. They must have shut down the security cameras before moving on to the library.

A quick check drew a frown. According to the log, they only shut down the recording, not the cameras themselves. They also checked on the status of a mothballed Kincade property, an alchemy lab set up on the outskirts of Central. The lab's purpose wasn't stated, which suggested one of the many Kincade black sites where they performed research of dubious legality.

Such precise searches implied a familiarity with the system. That combined with Malice's code meant they were almost certainly dealing with an inside job.

Artyom vastly preferred dealing with external threats. When your own people betrayed you, it was hard to know who you could trust.

Of course, his preferences meant nothing. He would deal with whatever he had to.

Leaving the computer room behind, he made his way down to the library. Four missing books from the dark magic section. That couldn't be good. What he couldn't figure out was why they'd come here to take them. There had to be less well-guarded collections they might rob. It argued once more for insiders.

Settling in front of the library computer he pulled up the log. The thief had done a search for books on demon summoning and binding. As he'd thought, definitely not good. There were eight total, so four must not have been useful.

He printed out the list, stood, and made the short walk to the dark magic section. There were four empty slots on the shelves. According to the list, all on advanced demon binding.

It would've taken only seconds to yank a bunch of books off, thus making it harder for him to figure out what was stolen. Did arrogance or haste keep the thief from taking even that much of a precaution? He didn't know and in the end decided it probably didn't matter.

Having learned all he could, Artyom marched out of the building and climbed back into his car. Once inside he pulled out his cellphone and dialed Ms. Kincade. He had a strong hunch his next stop was going to be that lab outside Central.

———

The alchemy lab where Malice experienced one of her greatest successes as a wizard and one of her greatest failures as a businesswoman looked exactly the same as she remembered, at least from the outside. The single-story warehouse officially served as a storehouse for hazardous chemicals. And it was, though the chemicals in question were actually alchemy reagents. A chain link fence secured with nothing but a chain and padlock prevented access.

Malice glanced around at the rundown neighborhood surrounding the warehouse. Graffiti covered the buildings and many of the windows had been boarded up. She'd chosen this location for more than the low cost of real estate. If an accident happened, no one that mattered would care how much damage it caused. It was a miracle no one had tried to break in and rob the place.

Not that massive drums filled with reagents would be an easy sell. In fact, if someone that didn't know what they were doing tried to open one, they were apt to kill themselves by breathing the fumes. Given her current status as a demon, Malice at least didn't have that to worry about.

"What a dump," Miguel said. "What could we possibly find in a place like this that would be of use to the mission?"

"You'll see soon enough. Come on."

She led the way across the parking lot where they'd appeared to a small side door. It was locked of course, but yielded quickly to her magic. Inside, the drums were stacked all over the place. She'd need the contents later, but for now she ignored them and went straight to the center of the building where a perfectly square opening had been left empty.

When Miguel joined her, she tapped a particular spot with her toe in a specific sequence. A rumble ran through the floor and the elevator they were standing on began to descend. Lights flashed on, revealing four glass tanks covered with drop cloths. Between each of the tanks sat a generator of sorts. Three empty tables and a pair of shelves laden with alchemy equipment completed the decorations.

"I saw the movie Frankenstein years ago at the village community center," Miguel said. "The mad scientist's lab looked much like this. Are we making monsters?"

"Monstrous thralls, yes. It's a remarkable process. Let's get everything uncovered."

It didn't take long to remove the tarps covering the tanks. A simple detection spell confirmed that the glass remained undamaged. Malice moved on to the generators. Everything looked intact. So far so good.

"What do those do?"

She hadn't noticed Miguel move to stand behind her. "They condense and distribute magical energy, what we now call the ether."

"There's technology that can interact with magic?"

"Not exactly. You can't see it from the outside, but inside the metal enclosure is a crystal set in a rune circle. Once a wizard provides the starting flow, the magic activates. The circle draws in ether, charging the crystal, which then discharges the energy through special magical conduits."

"You mean the jumper cables? I had a set of those back home for when my boat motor wouldn't start. It happened far too often."

"Magical jumper cables, I suppose that's close enough for our purposes. I need to begin the charging process. Once that's underway, we can gather the correct reagents from upstairs and begin the prep work."

"How long will it take to create the monsters?" Miguel asked.

"Since we don't need them to be smart or human looking, a rough protoform should take about twenty-four hours. Then we'll need to summon a demonic spirit to change it into a thrall. Lastly we repeat the process until the reagents are used up. That should give us a modest force of quite powerful servants."

Miguel slumped, a little frown on his lips. "Then we're going to be here for some time. I had hoped we might move quickly on to building a new temple."

"That's going to be a large undertaking. We don't even have a construction site picked out. It needs to be somewhere remote, so we can work in peace. Outside the Alliance at a minimum."

"Can we at least bring a new Black Eternal here? It would be a great help in transforming the thralls."

Malice bit back a scathing reply. Losing her temper at his every display of ignorance would only slow things down. "The two rituals would interfere with each other. Plus we need to gather sacrifices to power the summoning. Even in this neighborhood, if a bunch of people went missing, someone would notice."

Miguel clenched his fists, his whole body tense. "I've spent so much time running and hiding. Now I'm eager to get back to my mission."

Malice couldn't hold back a chuckle. "You've been hiding for about as long as I've been dead. The blink of an eye in the grand scheme of things. We're both basically immortal now; the one thing we have in abundance is time. As long as we survive and make progress, the master will be pleased. And in the end, that's the most important thing."

"You're right, I know that. But it's so hard to be patient. I had a taste of real power in Miami. People feared me. I had hundreds of thralls at my command. For the first time in my life it felt like I was somebody, something more than a nameless fisherman. And I want that feeling back."

Part of her new job, it seemed, was serving as this fool's therapist. Malice had a great many things she didn't want to do and this sat right up near the top of the list. But as had become clear to her, what she preferred and what she had to do didn't perfectly line up anymore.

"You'll have it back. But it'll take time, maybe even years. You don't have to like that fact, but it is a fact all the same. The first step on the road to recovering your power is right in front of us. Shall we take it together?"

"Yes. What do I do?"

Malice smiled. "I need to begin the charging cycle. Can you go back up and collect the drums we need for the first batch? We need two marked with a pair of inverted triangles that form a mark that resembles an hourglass and two marked with what looks like a horizontal figure eight."

"The barrels look quite heavy. Is it permissible to summon help?"

"By all means, do what you must. Simple spells won't interfere with the magic, only something more powerful and complex." Malice snapped her fingers. "I almost forgot."

She went over to one of the tables and grabbed a remote control. It only had two buttons, one marked with an up arrow and one with a down arrow.

"Here, this will let you control the elevator."

He took the remote and strode over to the lift. As soon as he did, Malice put the boy out of her mind. She'd done her babysitting for the moment. It was time to get to work.

———

Miguel rode the lift back up to the warehouse. His toe tapped as he muttered curses in Spanish. He knew he lacked the knowledge and skill to help with the finer aspects of the magic, yet he felt like he'd been reduced to little more than a laborer. Back home, laborers occupied the lowest rung of society. They worked for pennies, barely making enough to keep from starving. Even fishermen looked down on them. Not that fishing wasn't a hard life, but Miguel had owned his boat and kept what he made when he sold his catch. Some days that was nothing, but good or bad, the results came from his wit and determination.

Laborers just showed up and did as they were told. Just like he was now.

On the other hand, his dissatisfaction had to be weighed against getting in the way and ruining something with the potential to create many powerful servants. In the end, there was really nothing to think about. His feelings were irrelevant. If he needed to play the part of a laborer, then, for now at least, he would play that part.

The lift clunked into place and Miguel strode over to the nearest drum. It had the triangle mark. Out of curiosity he tried to lift it. The barrel didn't even budge. It had to weigh at least three hundred pounds. He could enhance his strength and lift it easily enough, but why dirty his hands when he had other options?

Focusing his will, he pointed at an open spot on the floor. A crimson circle appeared and black vines shot out, twisting and knotting into a four-legged body with two vine tentacles jutting out of it as big around as Miguel's body.

At his mental command it lifted the first barrel and set it on the elevator.

Miguel smiled. This was better. He felt like a manager now instead of a laborer. Nothing but word games to soothe his ego, but that was fine.

Mood improved, he quickly found and loaded the last four drums. With a press of the button he and his creation rode back down to the lab. Sparks were shooting off of the metal generators while Malice sat in a stone chair that appeared grown from the floor, one of the books she took from the library in her hand.

"You're reading while I work?" His annoyance came through loud and clear and he cursed his lack of self-control.

"The crystals are charging. I can't do anything else until they're finished, which will be in about three hours. You had no trouble finding the barrels?"

"No. I couldn't find any that weren't marked with either the triangles or a figure eight."

"That's because there aren't any others. Those two chemicals are the only ones required for this task. But they're kind of scattered around rather than divided into neat groups. I never did ask the lab manager why that was." She got a distant look in her eyes as if she was remembering something from long ago. It passed as quickly as it appeared. "Anyway, we've got three hours if you want to rest or practice your magic or whatever. I'll be studying these texts in hopes of finding something of use."

Miguel had no desire to practice at the moment, so he transformed his pet into a chair and sat down. He had grown thoroughly sick of waiting during his time with the druids, but it seemed he'd need to do at least a little more before he could finally see what his new monsters would look like.

Miguel smiled to himself. He could hardly wait.

16

C onryu emerged from a hell portal in a parking garage across the street from a four-story building. The bottom floor was a restaurant specializing in comfort food. According to the intel Mr. Kane provided, Alister Bund pretended to be a restaurant magnate, and actually owned over one hundred locations across the Alliance. He apparently used the restaurants to launder money, both his and other criminals'. That was probably how he and Cadus met. Much like with his friend, there was a great deal of difference between what the authorities knew and what they could prove.

The top three floors of the building served as the corporate headquarters for Bund Inc. A powerful magical barrier prevented entry via portal. He could smash it of course, but that would draw far too much attention. Much as he hated pussyfooting around, for now there was no other choice.

He walked out of the garage, an invisible Prime at his shoulder, and waited for the light to change before crossing the street. A glance through the windows as he approached confirmed that the diner was packed.

Inside, a woman behind a lectern smiled at him. She wore a

blue uniform with a white apron which matched the awning outside. "Table for one?"

Conryu's eyes flashed white as he channeled light magic into them and the greeter's expression went a bit slack. He'd learned this trick during his time with the vampires. Duplicating their mind-controlling gaze with light magic had been fairly simple. And useful as well; it didn't require any flashy movements or chanting. Normal people couldn't even imagine resisting it.

"I was hoping to speak with Mr. Bund."

"I'm sorry, sir, I can't help with that. Would you like to speak with the manager?"

"Please."

"Follow me." She led him deeper into the restaurant.

The babble of voices filled the air along with clattering silverware. The food smelled wonderful and his mouth watered when a server in blue and white walked by with a laden tray. Bund might be a scumbag, but his place seemed nice. If he ever got a day off, maybe he could bring Maria here for lunch.

There was an office behind the kitchen and the greeter knocked.

A middle-aged man dressed in a gray suit opened the door and glared at them. "What are—"

Conryu's mind control spell hit him mid-rant and he fell silent. Conryu turned to the greeter. "Go back to your post and forget you ever saw me."

She turned and walked away without another word.

"Let's talk in your office."

"Of course, sir. Please come in." The manager stepped aside and Conryu went into the office.

The room itself wasn't terribly impressive. A desk with a computer on top took up most of the space. There was also a filing cabinet and a chair for guests. What did impress Conryu was the stacks of money covering the desk. There had to be a hundred grand in cash.

"The restaurant business pays better than I thought."

"Oh, no, sir. This is cash from one of our clients. We'll run it through our business over the course of about a week before making a 'purchase' from our client thus returning it to him nice and legally."

"Fascinating, but I need to speak with Mr. Bund."

"Unfortunately, Mr. Bund is on an extended holiday with a dear friend of his. I have no idea when he'll return. Perhaps there's something else I can help you with?"

"Do you know his friend's name?"

"That would be Mr. Cadus, a longtime client of our business."

"Figured." Conryu helped himself to a stack of twenties. Normally he didn't like to steal, but since it belonged to criminals, he didn't feel too bad about it. "Return to your work and forget I was here."

"Very well, sir. Good day."

Conryu pocketed the money and walked out along the same path he followed inside. No one paid him the least attention. When he reached the garage he shifted to Hell. Kai and Cerberus were waiting.

"That was disappointing," Prime said.

"But hardly surprising." He absently patted Cerberus's flank as he thought. No matter how he looked at it, his only option was to investigate Fists of Steel's basement. That would have to wait until tonight, when the place was empty.

"What now, Chosen?" Kai asked.

"We've got a few hours before dark and I have a couple of questions for Mr. Kane."

An effort of will shifted them to the hall outside Mr. Kane's office and Conryu stepped out. Amy looked up at him as he rounded the corner. "Mr. Koda. Maria not with you today?"

"No, not today. Some things have come up and I need to talk to Mr. Kane."

She looked back down, checking the planner on her desk. No

way was she going to make him wait. He refused to consider the possibility.

"Looks like he's free for another half hour. Just a sec." She pressed the intercom on her desk. "Mr. Koda's here to see you, Chief."

"Send him right in."

"You can go ahead."

Conryu nodded and marched past her. A single knock on the door preceded his opening it. Mr. Kane stood behind his desk, his gray suit perfectly pressed and his bald head shining in the sunlight. They shook hands and he gestured to the chair in front of the desk.

"What brings you by?" Mr. Kane asked.

"You mentioned another department was investigating Cadus. Are they investigating Bund as well?"

Mr. Kane hemmed and hawed, looking anywhere but at Conryu.

"I'll take that as a yes. I stopped by his place of business today. The manager had a hundred grand in cash on his desk that he was planning to launder." Conryu placed the twenties he'd collected on the desk. "I helped myself to a few bucks. Since I haven't been able to make bikes, funds are getting low. Anyway, I got to thinking, don't you people sometimes pass marked bills to prove money laundering? I didn't want to get caught spending planted money."

Mr. Kane shot him a look then spread the money on his desk. "If you're low on funds, you should've said something. I could pay you out of petty cash."

"I'd just as soon avoid owing the government any favors."

"We really are on the same side." Mr. Kane took a light out of his desk and flipped it on. When he passed it over the bills, two of them glowed. "You were right to bring these to me. I'll return them to major crimes. You can keep the rest."

Conryu stood and collected the money. "You know, if you

were straight with me from the start, I'd be more likely to think well of the government."

"It's not so simple, son. I'm not the top of the food chain here. I take as many orders as I give. Talking out of turn to a civilian, even one as important as you, could land me in hot water. I know the demon lord thing is important, vital even, but that doesn't stop the rest of the world's problems. Criminals still need arresting, diplomacy goes on, that's just the way it is."

"You might be right, but I promise you that if my mission fails because you kept secrets from me, your criminal problems will seem like jaywalking in comparison. See you later."

Conryu opened a hell portal and vanished through it. That had gone about as well as he expected. It was pretty clear that Mr. Kane had no intention of being totally honest with him.

"Min."

The ninja on duty appeared before him along with the demon he'd summoned. The creature looked a bit like a bat with no eyes. According to Prime, out of all the demons in Hell, this kind had the best hearing.

"How may I serve, Chosen?" she asked.

"I think we're going to have to be a bit more aggressive in our observations. In addition to listening in, I'll need you to read his emails and any physical correspondence he might get. I know this is a big job, so we'll be arranging some reinforcements for you. Kai, could you pick out a couple girls to help?"

"Yes, Chosen." Kai hurried away. It wouldn't take her long to grab a couple Daughters and return.

"A question if I may, Chosen?" Min asked.

"Go ahead."

"Is Mr. Kane our ally or our enemy?"

Conryu smiled a sad little smile. "Usually he's our ally and he certainly isn't an enemy. The problem is, his bosses don't always appreciate the danger they might cause by keeping secrets. Given what they do for a living, it's an occupational hazard. Spying on him may actually make his job easier. I won't have to ask him questions he can't answer. It's an annoying workaround, but that's life."

She bowed. "Understood. Thank you for indulging me."

"Not at all. Anytime you have questions, ask them. I'd much rather explain something in more detail than have you uncertain what you should do."

Kai chose that moment to return with a pair of ninjas in tow. Both of the new arrivals stood at rigid attention. As always when they were wearing their uniforms, the girls looked virtually identical.

"This is Jen." Kai pointed at the right-hand ninja. "And her partner is Yung. They only completed their training two weeks ago and I thought this would be an easy first mission for them."

"Great, Kai, thanks. You two can relax." Despite his reassurance, both of them remained stiff as boards. "I need you to help Min keep an eye on Mr. Kane. It'll probably be a tedious task, so feel free to swap out with another pair whenever you want a break. I'll need a report every few days at minimum. If something important comes up, contact me at once. Most importantly, do not reveal yourselves. If there's trouble in the building, let Melina's team handle it unless it's a matter of life and death. Okay?"

"Yes, Chosen," Yung said.

"We will not fail you," Jen added.

"I'm sure you won't and thanks for your help."

All three members of the observation team bowed and Conryu willed himself and Kai to the vicinity of Fists of Steel. He'd find a place in the real world to wait for dark. That would be faster than staying in Hell.

"Will you tell Maria about the spies?" Kai asked.

He nodded. Conryu refused to keep secrets from Maria. Once he started, he'd never stop.

"She probably won't like it, but eventually one of Mr. Kane's secrets is going to get us into trouble. I can't risk it."

As usual Kai made no comment, either of approval or disapproval. On this occasion at least, he would've appreciated a bit of reassurance.

Putting Mr. Kane and his subterfuges out of his mind, Conryu began mentally preparing himself for tonight. All his instincts said it was going to be a bad time.

17

An hour passed far too quickly and Jonny found himself once more in the fighters' box watching as two men stood facing each other on the sand with Loong between them. It was Santana and... Shit, he'd forgotten the brackets. Anyway, a big black guy with an Afro that made it look like he'd been struck by lightning and enough muscles that if fighting didn't work out, he could always find work as a body-builder. The crowd was quiet around them, but it was an electric quiet, as if they were primed to erupt.

While they waited for the wizards to emerge and grant the fighters their power, Jonny glanced at the surviving fighters. None of them had spoken to him or Lala after their fight. It was like they feared to associate with somebody who had broken the rules of the tournament. Though calling them rules was probably overgenerous. It wasn't like Jonny had been disqualified for not killing Lala. He suspected that had more to do with Asterion's whims than anything.

At last the wizards appeared, one in black and the other in a blue bikini. This would be the first time someone had received dark magic and Jonny was curious to see how it worked out for them. Dark magic was Conryu's specialty, though he doubted anyone here came even close to his friend's skill in wielding it.

Santana ended up getting dark magic while his opponent got water. Jonny leaned forward, eager to see how they used them.

"Same rules as before," Loong said. "Fight until one of you is dead. Use the magic however you can. Ready? Begin!"

Loong hurried toward the exit tunnel, but Jonny ignored him. Santana hurled a black bolt of energy at his opponent, who dodged and flung an icicle back at him.

Jonny tugged on the nearest fighter's sleeve. When the man turned to glare at him he asked, "What's the black guy's name again?"

"Tyrone. You couldn't be bothered to kill your opponent, could you at least make an effort to learn our names? Fucking amateur."

Jonny winced, but he was technically an amateur when it came to this sort of fighting. It helped that he couldn't have cared less what these murderous lunatics thought about him.

He refocused on the fight and found Tyrone slashing at Santana with a blade made of ice.

Santana proved quick and elusive, but he still bled from several small cuts. At least he hadn't used up all his dark magic. Unlike the first round, both men seemed inclined to hold some of their power back. Leave it to top-level fighters to make the adjustment quickly.

The problem, for them at least, was that neither man seemed to understand exactly how the magic worked. Hardly surprising since they were bare-knuckle brawlers up until the tournament started.

Jonny's biggest advantage was the stuff he'd learned from Conryu as well as during basic training. A week on the fundamentals of magic might not seem like much, but right now he was pretty sure that training would save his life.

Santana sent a wave of darkness rolling toward Tyrone. When it hit his sword, the weapon vanished like it had never been.

Tyrone's moment of surprise cost him as he took a black-shrouded fist to the side of the head. Black flames exploded out on impact, turning Tyrone's head into a spray of bone and brains. Ugly but effective.

A servant led Santana off the sand and the stretcher-bearers carted the body away. Ten minutes later the next pair took their turn facing off. The fights took only half as long this time and sooner than he would've liked, Jonny found himself back on the sand. This round he faced a tall blond man that looked like Thor's second cousin with a huge tattoo of a rune hammer on his chest. His name was Carl, Jonny finally remembered.

Much as he would've liked it, getting earth magic a second time seemed unlikely. From his position between the two fighters, Loong favored Jonny with an angry, narrowed-eyed glare. Why did he care so much about whether Lala lived or died? His emotional reaction made no sense to Jonny.

"Alright," Loong said. "You two are the last ones for this round. Try and give the crowd a decent fight. And end it properly this time."

Jonny had expected this to be directed at him, but Loong was looking right at Carl when he said it.

The women emerged and this time the babe in black went to Jonny while Carl got red. When his wizard raised her hands a chill ran down Jonny's spine. The dark energy filled him with a mixture of desire and loathing. He'd never felt anything like it and found he wasn't a fan.

Across the way, Carl's hands were surrounded by the strange reddish-black flames that his wizard favored. He raised them in a boxer's stance and the way the flames surrounded his fists reminded Jonny of boxing gloves.

Though he would've preferred earth magic, dark magic was

his second-best option, if only because he'd spent a fair amount of time watching Conryu use it.

He knew exactly how to protect himself from Carl's magic.

"Ready? Begin!" Loong retreated for the tunnel as soon as he spoke.

Jonny pictured the darkness surrounding him an instant before a stream of flames hit him and fizzled.

This spell was called Cloak of Darkness and it worked like Stone Skin only it blocked magic instead of physical attacks.

Jonny charged, with no fear of any magic.

Carl tried blast after blast to equally little effect.

Either he wasn't the sharpest knife in the drawer or he was trying to burn away Jonny's protection.

A heavy right hook came swooping in toward Jonny's head.

He dodged.

Before Carl had a chance to recover, Jonny darted in and touched his right leg.

Dark magic surged out, draining the life from his flesh and withering the leg to a third of its former size.

Carl collapsed.

Jonny pounced and three hard rights to the head left the giant blond man out cold.

Loong stalked onto the sand as Jonny released the darkness that had been surrounding him. He looked no happier with the results this time than he had last time. Jonny found Loong's displeasure amusing.

"Head back for healing."

That was it, no threats, no gun, no nothing. Jonny shrugged and strode back the way he'd come. He'd barely reached the tunnel when a single gunshot rang out.

He spun around in time to watch Loong holster his weapon and the stretcher-bearers emerge to collect Carl's body. It seemed Asterion had decided that if Jonny wasn't going to finish the fights, he'd have Loong do it.

Disgusting as he found it, he didn't really know Carl and had a hard time feeling bad about the death of a murderer. Was he getting desensitized to the bloodshed? Perhaps. Jonny had no choice but to admit that, if only to himself.

He gave a little shake of his head. Once he got out of here, he'd be back to normal. Jonny had to believe that.

———

Asterion smiled to himself as Jonny strode out of the arena. From his place in the arena's solitary box, he'd watched all the fights, and dreary affairs they were, at least until the last. The boy had great potential, vastly more than any of the other so-called warriors in his tournament. He also had an excess of morality, but that was already fading. He'd made no effort at all to save the life of his last opponent.

In the next round he'd kill the man himself, hopefully.

"Why does that human interest you so, Master?" Cadus asked. "He seems too soft to me."

"His potential is what interests me. Did you see how he created a near-perfect imitation of Cloak of Darkness? He's seen magic used often enough to mimic it. His military training would also be useful. But most of all, turning a friend of the Reaper's Chosen to the Horned One's service would be sweet irony."

"But will he turn?"

"Time will tell. I have several ideas that may compel him in our direction."

The door behind him opened and Bund forced his bulk through. "Master, we may have a problem."

"What sort of problem?"

"The Reaper's Chosen showed up at my corporate headquarters an hour ago. He spoke to the manager and knows that Cadus and I are on vacation together."

"And how does that knowledge hurt us?" Asterion asked.

"I don't think it does, but security followed him until he vanished. Given the danger, they checked our camera network and spotted him again, this time sitting at a cafe across the street from Fists of Steel. He appears to be just waiting, likely for the place to close so he can investigate further. Should he find the teleportation circle…"

Asterion tapped his chin. "Hmm. That might, indeed, be a problem. We're getting close to the finals. Can't very well have an uninvited guest show up and ruin things. Take six of the Horned Guards and deal with him. I'll erase the circle after you're through."

"Do you think six will be enough?" Bund asked. "This is the Reaper's Chosen we're talking about."

"I don't expect you to defeat him. Just weaken him. I doubt a single battle will be enough to best him even if we sent all our forces."

"What if I'm destroyed?"

"What if you are? You'll be reborn in the master's hell, no worse for the defeat."

"The master may judge me a failure and end my existence."

Asterion rounded on Bund, his anger darkening the box. "If you keep arguing with me, I might judge you a coward and send you back myself."

"Forgive me, Master. I'll gather the warriors and await you at the circle."

"That's better." Asterion turned back and crossed his arms.

"How will Bund and I return to keep up our mortal disguises?" Cadus asked.

"You won't. Until things are settled, Mr. Cadus and Mr. Bund will be out of service. Losing their resources will be a nuisance, but a minor one in the grand scale of things."

Cadus lowered his gaze in acceptance, like a proper servant should. His partner could learn a thing or two from him.

Conflict with the Reaper's Chosen was inevitable, but he'd hoped to delay it until he found and empowered a hellpriest.

Oh well. A slow, evil smile spread across Asterion's face. The rest of the demon lords would soon see why the Horned One was the strongest of them all.

He'd hang the flayed skin of the Reaper's Chosen over the altar of his master's first temple.

18

Conryu sipped his coffee and sent a glance across the street. Nothing out of the ordinary happening at the gym. He couldn't shake the fear that he was wasting his time sitting in a little cafe like nothing in the world was happening. Sitting still had never been his strength. But sometimes that was the job.

His biggest fear was that whatever had happened at the gym was done and he should focus on other avenues. Pity he had no other avenues at the moment. Not to mention that if nothing else was going on, why did whoever had Jonny leave the barrier up in the first place? He'd learned a fair few things over the last couple days, but nothing that added up to anything that important.

He was missing something and he hated it.

Conryu was considering his options when a ripple ran through the ether.

Master.

I felt it, pal. It came from the gym, right?

Without a doubt.

Looked like he'd been spotted. How, he had no idea. Kai would've noticed anyone watching him.

Whatever, at least now he didn't have to wait any longer.

The waitress, an older woman that sort of reminded him of his mother, hurried over as he stood. "Can I get you anything else?"

"I'm good, thanks." He pulled a ten out of his pocket. "This cover it?"

"I'll get you some change."

"Keep it. The coffee was excellent."

She offered a bright smile. "Thank you, sir. Have a wonderful day."

He nodded and strode out onto the sidewalk. "I haven't sensed anything beyond that first burst of energy."

"Neither have I," Prime's disembodied voice said. "If whoever caused it knows you're here, it's likely they're setting a trap."

"That's a problem, but it gives us time to plan. Kai, head to the monastery and get some reinforcements. Depending on what we run into, a dozen extra swords will be welcome."

He didn't need her confirmation to know his order would be carried out.

A small group of people were coming down the sidewalk towards the cafe. Conryu crossed the street to get out of their way. A crazy person standing outside talking to himself by their front door wouldn't do the business any favors.

Kai appeared beside him. "We are ready, Chosen."

"Good, stay sharp. I don't know what we're walking into."

She vanished as quickly as she'd appeared, and Conryu walked right up to the gym and pushed through the door. A dozen people were working out at various stations, none seeming in the least aware of the danger beneath their feet.

"None of them are wizards," Prime said as he faded into view. "Ordinary people would at best have experienced what happened as a vague psychic chill and even then, they'd have to be especially sensitive to the flow of ether."

"Well, sensitive or not, they need to get out of here." Conryu moved well away from the door and loosed a fear spell.

People screamed, dropped whatever they were doing, and raced headlong for the exit. The group was small enough that no one got trampled in the rush.

When they were gone, he asked, "Is that everyone?"

Kai appeared. "Yes, Chosen. We searched the rest of the building and found no one else. The barrier blocking us from entering the basement is still in full effect."

"I'll have to do something about that. Thanks, Kai."

She offered a little bow and vanished again.

"How do you intend to handle this?" Prime asked.

"Unless you have a better suggestion, I thought I would go with a direct approach."

"You always go with the direct approach. But in this case, I can't think of anything better."

In Conryu's experience, the direct approach was almost always the best way to go. On the far side of the gym he found the door to the basement. The barrier appeared to begin at the bottom of the steps. He paused halfway down, called the Staff of All Elements to his hand, summoned a massive orb of dark magic, and loosed it.

The barrier hardly even resisted before dissolving into sparks of magic that quickly faded away.

"I sense demons," Prime said as soon as the sparkles had vanished. "And not the kind that work for you."

"That pretty much confirms that a hellpriest is involved with this fight-club business. I expected as much, but it never hurts to be sure."

Conryu resumed his descent and at the bottom found a large open area where six minotaur demons and perhaps the fattest human he had ever seen waited. The man wore a white suit with a too-tight red necktie. This had to be Bund.

"I don't suppose I can convince you to tell me where the fighters have been taken?"

Bund shook his head, jowls flapping back and forth as he did. "My master would be most displeased with me should I do so."

"Figured you'd say that." Conryu leveled the staff and the crystal at the tip turned white with an orange core. "Last chance to end this peacefully."

Bund's face twisted and he started to swell. Soon he had grown to twice his previous size and his skin was stretched tight. Even then the growth didn't stop. His skin split, revealing a scaly green... something underneath.

"A demon was wearing Bund's skin as a disguise," Prime said.

"No kidding."

White flames roared forth.

Conryu figured Bund had to be the most powerful of the bunch and he hoped to take him out quickly.

For such a huge monster, he moved quickly, dodging the flames and taking only minor damage.

"Kill him!" Bund shouted.

The minotaur demons all rushed toward Conryu, horns lowered as if they planned to impale him.

Kai and her fellow ninjas chose that moment to appear, taking the demons from the side and slashing with their black iron swords.

Howls of pain rang out.

Content to leave the small fry to Kai, Conryu renewed his focus on Bund. The fat demon had backed far enough away that his spine was touching the rear wall.

A wall of white flames sprang up at Conryu's command, hemming Bund in on either side and limiting his options to charging straight ahead or trying to smash through the wall.

Bund roared in frustration and hurled a sphere of reddish-black flames at Conryu.

A burst of dark magic negated the attack.

For the second time, a wave of white flames rolled out of Conryu's staff.

Bund leapt through the right wall of fire in a desperate attempt to escape.

As soon as he hit the flames, Conryu sent more power into them, turning the wall into an inferno.

Screams of rage quickly turned into howls of anguish as his demonic essence was consumed by the white fire. Bund had no hope of escape and Conryu had no mercy for demons. In less than a minute nothing remained save a small spot of ash.

The silent basement confirmed that the ninjas had dealt with the minotaur demons. Conryu turned to find them all on their feet and seemingly unharmed.

Just to be sure he asked, "Does anyone need healing?"

No one indicated that they did and after a moment Kai said, "The demons were strong, but not especially fast or smart."

"Lucky for me you are all strong, fast, and smart. Thanks for your help today."

They all bowed and one whose voice he didn't recognize said, "It was our honor to serve you, Chosen. Do you wish us to remain on standby or should we return to the monastery?"

Conryu considered his options. If he had a target immediately in mind, he would've told them to wait, but he had no idea where he should look next and no idea how long it would take to figure out. "You can return to the monastery, but tell Kanna I said not to give you another assignment. Once I figure out where we're going next, I'll send Kai to get you."

The spokeswoman bowed. "As you command, Chosen."

They vanished, leaving him alone with Kai.

"The grandmaster was most pleased that you were willing to call in backup."

Conryu smiled. "Yeah, I don't know how many times I'm going to have to fight and I want to conserve as much power as possible. The running battle with the Pale Princess kind of drove that need home. Is Kanna still upset about her undercover mission?"

"Not visibly, she has too much self-control to display such weakness. But inside, I can't say."

"I'll get her something nice to make up for it." Turning to Prime, Conryu asked, "I don't suppose you can figure out how to backtrack them from here?"

"No, Master. Whatever teleportation magic they were using has been completely erased."

"Well, shit." Conryu snapped his fingers. "Then again, maybe not. We found that weak temple on Crete and it was defended by demons just like these. I wonder if there are any other locations associated with the legend of the Minotaur."

Conryu opened the library door.

"Are we going to do research?" Kai asked.

"No. If we want answers sometime this century, we'd best leave it to someone that knows what they're doing. We're going to see Maria."

19

The private jet set aside for his use got Artyom from the West Coast to the Kincades' private runway near Central in an hour and a half. As he'd assumed, once he'd reported his progress to Ms. Kincade, she told him to do whatever he needed to in order to deal with the thieves. If either of her predecessors told him that, Artyom would've assumed that meant find the thieves, kill them, and dispose of the bodies. He didn't make that assumption with Kelsie and decided to do his best to capture the thieves alive. As long as he could do so without putting his own life in danger.

The jet taxied to a stop and he descended to the waiting black sedan. There was no sign of whoever had dropped it off for him. The Kincade security apparatus worked as efficiently as always. There should also be a team on standby so that once he confirmed the thieves were actually present, they could move in quickly.

He climbed behind the wheel and pressed the ignition. The central console lit up and he punched in the lab's address. Of course it was on the opposite side of Central from the airport. At least it was still early enough in the day that he would miss the evening traffic. He had driven through Central's rush hour on more than one occasion and was happy to avoid it whenever possible.

The city seemed peaceful from a distance as he drove along the four-lane highway that surrounded it. He shifted lanes and prepared to pull off as he neared his exit.

That was an illusion of course. Generally, in Central, the fights took place out of sight in the many government offices and corporate boardrooms. Every once in a while some lunatic tried to blow it up or burn it down, but that was, happily, the exception rather than the rule.

He pulled off the highway and only a block from the offramp entered one of Central's rougher neighborhoods. And by rougher he meant the sort of place you shouldn't go unless you were heavily armed or very desperate. Artyom reflexively touched the pistol in his shoulder holster and nodded once.

The only people out on the streets at the moment looked like extras from a zombie movie. They staggered around, barely able to stay on their feet as whichever drug they were on transported them to a land far, far away. These shambling fragments of humanity numbered among the sadder sights he'd seen over the years. Not that he could do anything for them, more's the pity.

Around three o'clock he pulled into the warehouse driveway and parked in front of the locked gate. It didn't look like anything was going on at the moment, but given that the lab lurked in the basement, anything could be happening down there.

Or nothing at all. That was the point of making a scouting run before calling in the team.

Steeling himself, he put the parking brake on and climbed out. As chief of security, he had keys to every property the Kincades owned. His keyring would've looked right at home on the belt of a high school janitor.

His at least were all neatly labeled and he soon found the one he wanted.

The lock popped open and he swung the gate aside.

Not wanting to make any more noise than necessary, Artyom approached on foot. The warehouse didn't have many windows and he did his best not to pass in front of them. He reached the side door, paused, and held his breath.

Seconds passed. No alarms sounded and no one came running. So far so good.

Taking another key from his ring, he unlocked the door and peeked inside. Scores of drums blocked his view of the central elevator. None of the overhead lights had been turned on, but the sun shining through the few windows would let him see well enough until night.

Now the dangerous part.

He ducked through the door and moved with slow, silent steps toward the center of the building.

Every moment he expected something to happen and every moment nothing did.

It was impossible to say if anything was different. Visiting the lab struck him as an excellent way to end up dead. At last he reached a spot between barrels where the elevator platform was visible.

Looked like he was in for a stakeout.

But happily not a long one. A vibration ran through the floor and the elevator began to descend.

Artyom dropped to his stomach and peered between a pair of lower barrels.

When the elevator came up, a young man of Latino descent, assuming the skin color of his bare arms could be trusted, stood in the center of the platform. He wore a black robe and some sort of plant monster made of twisted vines waited beside him.

This had to be the second thief. Which likely meant the first was below. Targets confirmed, he settled in to watch.

When the elevator reached the top and clunked into place, the youth pointed at one of the barrels. His pet stomped over, wrapped its vines around a fifty-five gallon drum and lifted it like it weighed nothing. Didn't seem possible it was that strong, but his eyes didn't lie.

Artyom made a mental note to bring flame throwers and incendiary rounds when they raided the place.

No, on second thought, he'd confirm that the chemicals weren't flammable first. Blowing up the whole warehouse with his team inside was not the result he was looking for.

It took only ten minutes for the youth and the vine thing to gather what they wanted from the inventory and then descend back to the lab. As soon as they were out of sight, Artyom snuck out of the warehouse and returned to his car. When the door had closed and locked he relaxed a fraction.

He pulled out his phone and punched in the names he'd seen on the barrels. Alchemy reagents, he knew that already. Scrolling down he found the information he needed. They weren't flammable but the fumes were toxic. Could've been worse. Every team kept gas masks in their truck just in case. That would take care of any potential danger from leaks.

Satisfied, he closed the browser and selected a number from his contact list. A deep, gruff voice answered at once. "Sir?"

"Targets confirmed. Meet me on site. Equip flame units and incendiaries. One wizard, dark magic aligned."

"Understood, sir. We'll be there in fifteen."

The line went dead and he pocketed his phone. A quarter hour then he'd find out just who was dumb enough to mess with Kincade Industries.

Miguel sensed the human fleeing the warehouse as he descended. It would've been so simple to kill him. A mere thought and the vines would've torn him apart. Letting the spy go went against everything he understood about their mission. They were supposed to be operating in secret after all.

A faint thud signaled the end of his trip down. All four vats were bubbling away, as vaguely humanoid blobs took shape. They were completely full. Where was he supposed to put the stuff he brought down?

Malice sat off to one side, her nose buried in a book. She'd already skimmed one of them and tossed it aside in disgust. Whatever she hoped to find clearly wasn't there.

"Where do you want me to put these barrels?"

Malice looked up. "Anywhere off to the side. We won't need them until we start the second batch."

His lip twisted in a snarl that he quickly suppressed. "If we don't need them, why did you ask me to bring them down?"

"So the scout would see you and know that we're here. He wouldn't call in the rest of the team without that confirmation. That's standard procedure for Kincade security units."

Miguel ordered the vine beast to set the barrels out of the way. "If you knew he was here, why didn't you tell me?"

Malice cocked her head. "I assumed you'd sensed him as soon as he arrived, the same as I did."

"You assumed incorrectly. Explain to me why we want a security team to come here in the first place."

She closed the book and offered a long-suffering sigh. Miguel forced himself not to get annoyed. He assumed whenever he did, she was laughing silently at him.

"How much of basic summoning principles do you understand?"

Miguel shook his head. "I know I can summon the vines or plant beast with a thought and demons with greater effort."

"Essentially correct. When you summon them that way, your own magical power sustains them during their time in this world. If you run out of power, they vanish. There's a second method of summoning that is far more useful, but also more difficult. And that is using life energy from sacrifices. You need to transfer an amount of life force roughly equal to the power of the demon you want to summon. That way the demon can remain here without draining you."

"Like how I brought you here."

"Exactly. Since you did that, I assumed you understood the principles behind the magic. We need at least five people to bring a Black Eternal here from Baphomet's hell. That's the minimum number for a security team."

Miguel's jaw dropped. "You've been planning this since before we reached Kincade West."

"Yes. You sound surprised."

"I am. I mean, how could you know all this would happen the way you intended?"

"I know the way the system works. I wrote all the rules after all. Just enough clues remained behind to draw them here, but not so many that they'd know I left them on purpose. I lived for a long time as a frail old woman. Subtlety and manipulation were my tools even more than magic. Any idiot can charge in, magic blasting every which way. But getting your enemy to dance to your tune without them even realizing it, that's art."

If Miguel had briefly been foolish enough to underestimate Malice, he knew better than to do so now. She was so clever and so far ahead of him that he hardly dared try and think what else she might have in mind.

And for all he knew, planting these doubts in his mind might be what she intended by telling him all this. He could second-guess himself to death if he didn't take care.

"It won't take the security team long to arrive," Malice said, interrupting his thoughts. "Can I leave their capture to you?"

"Of course. What danger is a handful of normal humans to me?"

"Don't be arrogant. They'll have at least one wizard with them and we need them alive for the ritual to work. Oh, and do catch them outside the warehouse. We wouldn't want to damage any of our supplies."

"Anything else?" Miguel asked, his tone snottier than he intended.

Malice acted like she didn't even notice. "I can't think of anything."

Miguel stalked back to the elevator. He'd wait for the humans upstairs.

When he glanced back at Malice, she already had her nose stuck back in her book, Miguel clearly forgotten about.

And she told *him* not to be arrogant.

20

Jonny stood on the sand of the arena once again. His third-round match had been a bit tougher than the first two, but he came through with only a few scratches. He got wind magic last time, and had used it both to fly and to suck the air out of his opponent's lungs. For this round he was really hoping for light magic. If he could win without using all of it, hopefully he'd be able to use anything left over to heal Lala. With the tournament nearing its end, he feared if they didn't escape soon, they never would.

While they waited for the wizards to arrive to grant them their powers, Jonny studied his opponent for this round. He was an Asian man, perhaps ten years Jonny's senior. Shirtless and with a shredded physique, he kind of reminded Jonny of a younger version of Conryu's dad.

Hopefully he wasn't as skilled as Sho. Having to fight someone at the grandmaster's level, magic or not, would be bad for Jonny's health.

"Will you be going easy on me as well?" his opponent asked.

Jonny smiled at the question. He hadn't killed any of his opponents in the fight, but Loong had finished off the last two with a bullet to the back of the head. Given that, he wasn't sure that sparing them was much of a kindness.

"That depends on what you consider going easy. I certainly won't roll over and die for you."

"Your style of martial arts is interesting. Who is your master?"

"I didn't have just one. I started out with karate, added a bit of kung fu, and then mixed in a little military combat training. I suppose you could say I'm a bit of a mongrel martial artist."

"That is often the best way. Various styles can cover for each other's weaknesses." The wizards chose that moment to emerge from their tunnel. "It seems the time has come. Best of luck."

Jonny nodded back, but didn't speak. He couldn't wish his opponent luck and mean it. All Jonny wanted was to survive and escape with his friend. Nothing else mattered to him.

As he hoped, the wizard in white came to stand in front of him. The way he kept getting exactly what he wanted made Jonny think that someone could read his mind. That would also explain how Asterion knew his real last name.

It was an unsettling thought. It meant that no matter what he did, he had no hope of succeeding.

Johnny grimaced and tried to relax as the power flowed into him. He couldn't think that way. He could only try his best to escape. Otherwise he might as well just lie down and die.

A few feet away, his opponent, Jonny hadn't even bothered to learn the man's name, received fire magic. That seemed to be the most popular for some reason.

The wizards left the arena and Jonny found himself facing an opponent with black-tinged red flames dancing around his fists. Fire was a better matchup for him than dark magic, but he still had no intention of letting his guard down.

"Begin!" Loong shouted.

Jets of flame propelled Jonny's opponent right at him.

Jonny dodged by the slimmest of margins and fired a lightning bolt as he passed.

A wall of flames sprang up to block it.

It seemed Jonny wasn't the only one thinking about how best to use the magic.

His opponent emerged from behind the curtain of flames and hurled a ball of fire at Jonny.

He dove, rolled under the spell, and winced when it exploded, burning his back.

Light magic healed him an instant later and he sprang to his feet, fist leading.

A left-hand parry turned Jonny's strike aside.

Toe to toe, they exchanged a barrage of blows, each turning the other's attacks aside, the magic forgotten.

Well, not really forgotten. Jonny was just waiting for the right moment.

And it came in the form of a spinning back fist.

As soon as his opponent turned away, Jonny lashed out with more lightning.

At such close range, there was no chance for him to dodge.

The spell drove the unlucky man across the arena, slamming him face-first into the wall where he slid to the sand.

Jonny was on him in an instant.

Two hard, lightning-enhanced, hammer-fist blows left him out cold, the flames around his fists guttering to nothing.

He stood and assessed the damage he'd taken as well as how much power he had left. The answer to both questions was not much. Jonny had hoped to hold back more power, but there was no point if he lost. And he would have.

Loong emerged from the tunnel, pistol already drawn. He jerked his head toward the exit and Jonny walked off without a word. He should've at least tried to argue against the killing, but he knew it wouldn't do any good. It wasn't like Jonny was willing to do anything to force Loong to spare the unlucky fighter.

He reached the tunnel entrance before the gunshot sounded.

Maybe he was gutless for letting Loong do his dirty work.

Jonny was honest enough to admit that possibility. But at the end of the day, he just didn't have it in him to kill if his own life wasn't in danger. He really didn't know how someone could just walk up to an unconscious man and put a bullet into the back of his head like it was no big deal. A human shouldn't be able to do that.

A bitter smile twisted his lips as he stepped into the barracks. That was a joke. There were plenty of people walking the streets right now that wouldn't bat an eye at killing a helpless person. It sucked, but that was the truth.

Jonny found Santana staring at him from his bunk when he entered, his dark eyes narrow and intense. "You and me in the finals."

"Looks like."

Santana shook his head. "After seeing your first fight, I never thought you'd make it this far."

"I doubt you're the only one to think that."

Jonny stopped beside Lala and found his friend asleep. He put a gentle hand on his wrist and willed what power remained to flow into his friend's damaged body. Jonny couldn't heal everything, but he repaired the worst of it.

Sometime during the transfer Lala opened his eyes. "Survived again, I see."

"One more time anyway. How do you feel?"

"Better. Do I have you to thank for that?"

"I saved as much light magic as I could without risking a loss. I had hoped to do more."

Lala sat up and winced. "You did enough. Many thanks. At least when Loong kills me, I'll be able to face him on my feet."

"Why would he kill you?"

That brought a chuckle that resulted in another pained wince from Lala. "After everything that's happened, you can't imagine he'll just set me free? 'Off you go, Lala. Now don't tell anyone about the battles to the death you've taken part in.' No, my friend. Only the winner will walk out of here."

"And that's going to be me." Santana stood, arms crossed, glaring at the two of them. "I mean to claim that treasure and whatever else our host is offering."

Jonny didn't care about the prize, though he wouldn't turn his nose up at a pile of gold. It was the strings that were attached to the prizes that worried him.

Before he could say as much, Loong stepped into the doorway. "The bosses decided to give you half a day to recover before the final. Eat, rest, and behave yourselves. They want you in tip-top shape tomorrow."

With that brief announcement, Loong returned to wherever he came from. Santana shot them a final glare before marching out.

"A slight reprieve," Lala said.

"Slight being the operative word." Jonny looked around as if there was someone to overhear. "I didn't just heal you to ease your pain. I mean to make a break for it tonight. Are you coming with me?"

Lala nodded. "I'm dead anyway. Better to at least try and survive than wait like a steer in the slaughterhouse."

Jonny grinned and clapped him on the shoulder. They'd make it out of here together, he knew it.

21

The boxy, black battlewagon met Artyom half a block from the warehouse. The armored truck carried an arsenal along with computer surveillance equipment. The six-member team, five men and one woman, piled out and stood at attention in front of him. They were all fit and equipped with the latest body armor and weapons. Even the wizard wore ballistic armor and carried a sidearm. Most importantly they all had the emotionless expressions of stone-cold killers.

"You're late," Artyom said.

No one responded. Seventeen minutes was only two minutes off the standard response time but it suggested sloppiness and he wouldn't stand for that. At least they didn't compound the error by making excuses.

"We have two targets, a man and a woman. The woman is certainly a wizard. She's proven capable of wielding dark as well as earth magic. I don't know which is her aligned element. I also don't know her power level. Extreme caution will be needed. As for the man, we have no data on him. I estimate his age at twenty years. He's dressed in some sort of black robe which suggests a demon worshipper."

"Based on the facts you've presented," the wizard said. "Dark magic is the wizard's most likely alignment."

Artyom nodded. "That's my working theory as well. Is it going to be a problem?"

"Depends on her power level. I measured a hair over one thousand. If she's stronger than me, we could be in trouble. But wizards over a thousand are rare, so we should be okay."

"Right. Sound off."

The first man said, "Alpha One."

They went through Alpha Five then the wizard ended with, "Alpha Six."

"Good," Artyom said. "My comms designation is Leader. Let me gear up and we'll move. And don't forget masks, a stray shot could fill the warehouse with toxic gas."

He climbed into the back of the battlewagon and shrugged into a vest. As he worked on his leg armor Alpha One asked, "Are we expecting them to use comm scanners?"

"Them? Doubtful. But in this part of the city, you can bet there will be plenty of police scanners and I don't know about you, but I'd just as soon not have my name broadcast for the locals to hear."

"Gotcha, Leader."

Artyom strapped on a helmet and mask, slipped a pistol into a thigh holster, and grabbed a rifle from the rear rack. The final step was to slap a clip filled with phosphorus rounds into place and rack one into the chamber. After confirming the safety was on, he hopped out of the truck.

"Alpha One, you're on point. Six, you're with me in the center. Let's move."

They set out with One in the lead, weapons up and at the ready. Six's job would be to monitor the area for magical dangers and deal with them. Artyom hadn't run into anything dangerous on his first visit, but that was no guarantee. He might have just gotten lucky.

It didn't take long to reach the sedan. It sat untouched in the warehouse parking lot, the gate in front of it wide open.

"Leader, I've got movement near the warehouse entrance," One said.

Artyom shifted his gaze and quickly spotted the young man from earlier pacing outside the warehouse. Looked like he was waiting for something.

"Move in," Artyom said. "If he tries anything, drop him. Six, what's the magic situation?"

"Hard to tell. There's so much background energy swirling around the warehouse, I can't get a clear read on the grounds."

"Not what I wanted to hear."

The group slipped past his car and worked their way across the parking lot. The young man finally noticed them and crossed his arms.

"Finally. She said you'd be here sooner than this."

"On your knees, hands behind your head," One said.

The young man cocked his head to the right as if confused. "You're not actually policemen, right? What makes you think you can run around giving orders like this?"

"You're trespassing," One said. "Corporate security has the right to protect the company's property. Now, kneel!"

Still no reaction. For most people, having six rifles pointed at your chest encouraged rapid compliance. This kid seemed totally unimpressed.

The youth pursed his lips in thought. "This is all of you, right?"

"Watch o—"

The ground exploded all around them, rendering Six's cut-off warning pointless.

Vines wrapped Artyom from neck to ankles and lifted him off the ground.

The others received similar treatment. They'd been captured without even firing off a shot. Talk about pathetic.

He looked left and right, trying to spot the wizard. As far as he could tell, the young man was alone.

"Where's the magic coming from?" Artyom asked.

"From him." Six's voice trembled. "And he's strong. Vastly stronger than me. We're in serious trouble here."

Artyom hardly needed to be told that last bit. "I thought there was only one male wizard."

Before Six could answer, Artyom found himself being jerked toward the ground until he was nose to nose with the young man whose face had twisted in a hate-filled snarl.

"I am not a wizard and do not ever compare me to *him!*" Panting with rage, their captor continued. "I am a hellpriest of Baphomet and in time this world will belong to my master. Not that you'll be alive to see it."

The vines holding Artyom and his team pulled themselves free of the ground and transformed into plant beasts like the one the hellpriest had used to carry the barrels.

Artyom racked his brain as they were carried into the warehouse, past the stacks of barrels, and over to the elevator. He'd heard the word hellpriest or maybe read something about it in an email update. They were some kind of new magic user and damn little was known about the extent of their abilities.

They were also supposed to be rare. What were the odds of running into one here?

As they rode down to the basement, he struggled to get free of the vine pinning his arm to his body. Every movement only caused it to squeeze tighter until he could barely breathe. He did manage to scrape his mask off, but other than that accomplished nothing. Escape, it seemed, was not an option.

Not at the moment at least.

———

Malice paged through the final book she'd collected from Kincade West's library. An occasional vibration ran through the floor as the magic worked. The protoforms would be ready in about ten more hours. The systems were working exactly as intended despite having been shut down for nearly three decades.

The ether surged and a particularly heavy crash sounded outside. Sounded like the security team had finally arrived. When she reached the end of the book, she tossed it into the corner of the room with the first three.

Worthless, every one of them.

There had to be some way to free herself from Baphomet's control. Malice had always been the master of her own fate and she damn well wanted to be again. The books, however, claimed that demons, even one created using a mortal soul like Malice had been, were simple extensions of the Reaper's, or in her case Baphomet's, will. The demon lords had the power to create and destroy their minions whenever they desired. It was a horrid situation, nearly worse than simply being dead.

There had to be other places she might look for the secret. And look she would, all while playing the obedient servant and stringing the idiot hellpriest along.

Speaking of her "master," the elevator had begun its descent. Seven people were wrapped up in vines, two more than she expected. Had they changed the team parameters after she died?

Malice shook her head and stood. Let's see what they'd caught.

She strode over just as the elevator hit the bottom.

"I got them," Miguel said. "This lot didn't put up much of a fight."

"Dealing with weaklings when you have the element of surprise does make life easier."

"Malice?" one of the security officers said.

She moved closer. "Chief Gladyr. I hadn't expected to find you here. Surely Kincade Industries chief of security has better things to do than investigate a simple break-in."

"I was in the area and the thieves tried to use your old code. Now I know why. I thought you were dead."

"I was. Now I've been reborn as a demon. Though I suspect many people thought I was already one."

"You know this one?" Miguel asked.

"I do. Chief Gladyr is a loyal and trusted employee of my former company. Seems a shame to reward that loyalty by sacrificing him, but that's the way it goes. I truly do wish you hadn't come yourself, Chief."

Malice snapped her fingers and a wave of dark magic rolled over the bound prisoners. All their equipment and weapons rotted and rusted to nothing in seconds, leaving them dressed in little more than rags.

"What did you do that for?" Miguel asked. "They can't threaten us even with their weapons."

"True, but it was their communications equipment I really wanted to destroy. We have all the sacrifices we need for now and if they somehow managed to call in reinforcements, it would've been troublesome."

"Should I prep them for sacrifice?" Miguel asked.

"Not yet. The ritual will interfere with alchemy equipment. We've got about half a day to go, then we can begin."

"So what should I do with them?"

Malice made a vague shooing gesture. "Hang them from the back wall out of the way."

The vines obliged, leaving the wrapped-up security officers hanging like seed pods. Which wasn't so far from the truth depending on how you looked at it.

"Did you find what you were looking for?" Miguel nodded toward the pile of books.

"Unfortunately not. Once our position is more secure, I'll need to expand my search."

And she wouldn't stop searching until she found a way to be free again.

22

Conryu stepped out of his library and into the Department of Magic's research library. He'd called Maria ahead of time and she asked him to give her an hour to gather information on the Minotaur legend. He dearly hoped she found something because he was fresh out of ideas.

Kai followed him out and immediately vanished into the borderlands.

He sensed only one life force in the library and a short walk through the stacks brought him to Maria, who had her beautiful nose stuck in a three-inch-thick leather-bound book. He stepped extra loud in the hope that she'd hear him approaching. Much like his mother, she sometimes got annoyed when he appeared out of nowhere.

Three strides from her table she finally lowered the book and looked at him. Conryu grinned back. There wasn't a more beautiful woman in the world.

"Hey, anything good?"

Maria sighed and waved him into the chair beside hers. "The Minotaur is very much a legend of Crete. I can't find another solid reference. Since you destroyed the temple there, we can assume that the Horned One has a second temple elsewhere."

"That's reasonable," Conryu said. "I can find a pocket dimension pretty easily now, if you can give me a hint about where to look."

"The only other place I can think of is Athens. The hero that killed the Minotaur lived there. It's the only other city I can find directly mentioned in the legend."

"Okay, but Athens is a pretty big city. Any thoughts on where I should start?"

"The acropolis. That's where most of the intact ruins are. The area is basically a tourist trap now, but there might be an entrance hidden in some obscure corner of an ancient ruin. That's the best I can do. If you don't find what you're looking for in Athens, I'm out of suggestions."

Conryu kissed her cheek. "I appreciate the help."

His face twisted up and she asked, "What's wrong?"

"There's something I need to tell you and I'm afraid you won't like it."

"Tell me. It would hardly be the first time I didn't like something you had to do."

He blew out a sigh. "I've got two more girls keeping an eye on your dad as well as a demon with especially good hearing. His habit of keeping things I need to know a secret is an issue. They might not get all the details, but at least I won't be totally in the dark when something happens that he doesn't want to tell me about."

"I don't blame you a bit. Dad sometimes has too much politician in him and it keeps him from seeing the bigger picture. For example, that stopping a demon invasion might be more important than upsetting the president."

"So you're cool with it?"

"Yes. Do what you have to. He won't hear a word from me."

Conryu sagged with relief. "That's good to know. I feared my spying might lead to one of our occasional disagreements."

He pushed away from the table and stood. "Now that the unpleasant work is done, I need to go try and find Jonny. See you later."

"Good luck and be careful."

"I'll do my best, but in this line of work, being careful isn't always a possibility." With a final goodbye kiss, he opened the library door and stepped through.

An instant later he emerged on the top floor of the nearby parking garage. Kai joined him as soon as he appeared.

"Have they heard anything?"

"Nothing relevant to our current mission. There are mutters about increased heart hunter activity at the border. He also seems upset that the Seattle office failed to notice what was happening at the druid camp, but other than that, nothing's going on."

Conryu hadn't had anything to do with the heart hunters since his first year at the Academy. Given how little he knew about the elf-blooded freaks, he wasn't sure if he should be worried or not. In the end he decided to worry later. Finding Jonny was the priority for now.

"Okay, remind me to thank them when we wrap things up."

"You don't need to worry about thanking us, Chosen. Serving you is our duty."

"I know, but everyone appreciates a kind word and I really am grateful for everything you and the other Daughters do for me." Conryu opened a hell portal and stepped through. "Speaking of the others, do you mind grabbing our backup? I want them on standby in case we find something. I'll meet you in the border-lands above Athens."

Kai bowed and hurried away through the endless darkness.

Cerberus chose that moment to come trotting up. Conryu patted his flank and flew up on his back. "Prime, you can let the invisibility spell go now."

His familiar shimmered into view. Prime couldn't actually use that spell, but Conryu had made a simple magic ring and attached it to Prime's cover. Whenever he charged it with ether, the spell activated. It saved Conryu the trouble of constantly renewing the magic.

"Do you think we'll actually find anything in Athens?" Prime asked.

"Beats me, but unless you have a better idea, we're going to look."

"I don't, but I can't help thinking we're overlooking something. We destroyed that first temple with relative ease. It felt like a decoy, but the guardian demon must have come from there, which implies that it was the main temple. Trying to make sense of all this is making my head hurt."

"You don't even have a head."

Prime grumbled and fell silent, drawing a grin from Conryu. He scratched Cerberus's central head. "Okay, boy. Take us to Athens."

Cerberus leapt into action and soon it felt like they were flying through the darkness. After what seemed like a few seconds of running Cerberus stopped and barked once.

"Here already? Good boy."

He hopped down and opened a viewing window. Athens was a bustling city with people hurrying here and there, carrying bags or pushing carts. Cars honked and one cabby waved his fist at an old lady making her way across the street. It was every bit the modern city.

An effort of will shifted the view to the acropolis. Jutting columns filled the portal. He pulled back and found hundreds of people swarming around, taking pictures and generally acting like tourists. If a fight broke out here, not only would he need to worry about damage to Greece's cultural heritage, but also civilian casualties.

It wasn't the worst place he could imagine having a battle, but it wasn't far off.

He sensed Kai approaching and turned to see her and twelve Daughters of the Reaper rapidly closing the distance. When they arrived they all bowed.

"Thanks for coming, everyone. Here's the plan. I'm going to pop out and start searching for a pocket dimension. Assuming I can find one and figure out how to gain access, you will all join me and we'll enter. The goal is to destroy the guardian demon and the temple core. We also need to find Jonny."

"Which is the priority?" one of the Daughters asked.

"The demon and the temple core." Conryu hated himself a little for saying that, but when you weighed Jonny's life against the danger of a temple becoming fully consecrated, there really was only one choice. "Based on what I know about pocket dimensions, we might not even be able to gain access. If that happens, we'll need to stake out the location and strike when someone emerges."

"That was for a sealed temple," Prime said. "Since the guardian demon has already entered and brought others with him, the rules might be different."

"Let's hope so, pal. If anyone has a question, now's the time."

They all stared silently back at him. As usual they were ready to obey his commands without hesitation. Hopefully none of them came to regret their devotion.

"Okay, let's do this." Conryu wrapped himself in an invisibility spell, opened a portal, and stepped out into midair five hundred feet above the acropolis. A flying spell caught him before he'd fallen ten feet.

Taking a deep breath, he focused his attention on the magical realm. A pulse of light magic shot out in all directions. Only another wizard keeping close watch would notice anything and if they did, it would be clear the spell was harmless.

It also revealed nothing. If there was an anchor around here, it wasn't within his range.

Conryu flew to the edge of the spell and cast it again. The results were equally dim. The process continued until he'd checked the entire acropolis and found nothing of interest, magically speaking at least.

"This was a waste of time," Prime said.

"Not really. At least now we know the temple isn't in the acropolis."

He was debating where to look next when his phone rang. "Maria? I didn't expect to hear from you so soon. What's up?"

"I was reviewing the notes I made on the Minotaur legend. When you went to Crete, did you actually search the other sites I mentioned?"

Conryu slapped his forehead. "No. After we found the first temple, Kanna showed up and I got sidetracked by the Pale Princess business. I never even thought about it again."

"You might want to check them. That first temple you found might be like a fake nest."

"Fake nest?"

"Yeah, there are some species of bird that will make an obvious fake nest to distract predators from the real, hidden one."

"That would explain why the temple's guardians and its core were so weak," Prime said.

Conryu cursed clever demon lords, his patron excepted of course. "I'm headed for Crete. Assuming you're keeping track somewhere, you can make a note that the acropolis is demon free."

"I'm sure the Greek Historical Society will be happy to hear that. Good luck."

"Thanks. I'll take all I can get."

23

K elsie sat at the desk in her mother's office at the mansion and tried to focus on the most recent profit-and-loss statements from the European division. The numbers swam before her eyes as her mind drifted to the last update she'd received from Chief Gladyr. The idea that some faction loyal to her grandmother's legacy still lurked inside Kincade Industries terrified her. This job was hard enough without having to worry about internal company politics.

She finally gave up, pushed away from the desk, and started pacing. It was still light out which meant very little time had passed since the last report. She really needed to relax and trust that the chief knew his business and would handle things appropriately. Kelsie was certainly not the best one to consult when it came to security.

The phone rang and she jumped a little before rushing to grab the handset. "This is Kelsie, go ahead."

"Ms. Kincade," a gruff man's voice said. "My name is Smith and I'm assigned to the Central security force. Chief Gladyr left orders to contact you if he was out of radio contact for more than thirty minutes. We haven't been able to reach him on any channel and as far as we can tell the system is dead. What would you like us to do?"

Kelsie ran a hand through her hair. This was the worst possible scenario. There was a serious threat, people were looking to her for answers, and she had no idea what to do.

"Did he say anything before the radio died?"

"The last word he sent was that the team had arrived on site and was about to breach the facility. We can confirm nothing after that. The second assault team is ready to investigate at your order."

She chewed her lip and finally said, "No. If the first team was, heaven forbid, taken out, we can't send another group to face the same fate. I'll find another way. In the meantime, if the chief contacts you, let me know at once."

"Understood, ma'am."

The line went dead and Kelsie hung up. There was only one person she could think of to call for help, but she hated to keep relying on Conryu. He had so much on his plate right now. The reason she took over Kincade Industries was to help him, not to cause him more grief.

She slumped in her chair. What was she going to do?

———

Jonny sat up in his cot and looked around the dimly lit dormitory. Santana was snoring away, seeming totally zonked out. Lala wasn't moving either, but hopefully he wasn't too out of it. Holding his breath and listening revealed nothing of interest. If they were going to go, now was the time.

With painful care, Jonny swung his legs off the side of his cot and slipped them into his boots. That didn't draw a reaction from Santana either. So far so good.

He tiptoed over to Lala and gave him a gentle shake. The man's eyes popped open and he stared at Jonny for a second before nodding. A little push nudged the still-injured man into a sitting position and Lala slid his feet into his own shoes. He paused halfway down to tie them and grimaced.

Jonny put a hand on Lala's shoulder, took a knee, and tied them for him. Together they eased over to the door. It let out a soft squeak when Jonny opened it, but Santana's snoring never wavered. Thank heaven for heavy sleepers.

A quick look up and down the hall confirmed that the coast was clear. When they'd put a dozen strides between themselves and the dorm Lala muttered, "This is pathetic. I haven't needed someone to tie my shoes since I was four."

"You're injured," Jonny whispered back. "Don't take it personally."

That comment brought even more disgruntled grumbling, this time in what Jonny assumed was Turkish since he couldn't understand a word of it. He cared a good deal less about the content than the volume, which Lala thankfully kept barely audible.

At the end of the tunnel they paused at the foot of the ramp that led to the arena. Still no sign that anyone was aware of their escape attempt. Of course, they hadn't gone anywhere they weren't supposed to yet. That all would change in a few more steps.

"Why do we wait?" Lala asked.

"Just checking to make sure Loong isn't up there with his gun. If I hear someone, we can always go back and try again in a few hours."

Lala shook his head. "It won't be any better then. Let's just go for it."

He had a point. Jonny shrugged and led the way up onto the sand. Seeing the arena empty and silent seemed strange. He'd gotten used to the cheers of the crowd. Two tunnels led out of the arena and into what he assumed was the guest area and hopefully the exit.

But which tunnel to take?

"Go right," Lala said. "The wizards came from the left and I don't want to run into them."

That worked for Jonny and he got moving. The right-hand tunnel was darker than the one that led back to the dormitory. Jonny stayed close to the wall, trailing his fingers along as he went. After five minutes, the passage showed no sign of stopping. How far away was the exit?

The answer came a few seconds later when he spotted a light directly ahead of them.

"Finally." Jonny picked up the pace a bit only to catch himself and look back at Lala.

"I'm fine. No need to baby me."

Jonny had his doubts about that, but decided to keep them to himself. The light grew brighter and the exit bigger as they got closer until finally they stepped once more onto the sands of the arena. Asterion and Cadus waited for them, along with two of the wizards, the fire one and the light one. The crowd once more filled the seats and they cheered as Jonny and Lala emerged.

"It's not possible. We were walking straight ahead."

"And where did all the people come from?" Lala asked.

That was a damn good question.

"Welcome, my friends," Asterion said. "It seems the final contest is going to happen earlier than I expected."

Loong emerged from the tunnel opposite them with Santana ahead of him at gunpoint. Nothing that was happening made any sense to Jonny.

"What the hell is going on?" he asked.

"What a perfect turn of phrase," Asterion said. "Hell is exactly what's going on. Specifically the search for a hellpriest to serve my master. I've chosen you, Jonny Salazar. Out of all the fighters here you have the most potential. Your basic understanding of magic is far ahead of your fellows and you have sufficient skill in combat."

"What about the treasure?" Santana demanded. "We were

supposed to fight it out for a chest of gold. What's this hellpriest horseshit?"

Loong pistol-whipped Santana across the back of the head, sending him crashing to the sand. "You will be silent when Master Asterion is speaking."

"Now, now," Asterion said. "He has a right to be upset. Promises were made. Granted, they were promises I never intended to keep, but nevertheless I can understand Santana's displeasure. The treasure was just an illusion, something to help motivate you greedy mortals. Becoming a hellpriest of the Horned One is the real prize. You will have power and eternal life. You will rule this world like a god."

Asterion took a step toward Jonny, a faint smile twisting his lips. "I know you want power. How long have you stood in Conryu Koda's shadow? With my master's power you will be able to fight him on equal footing. You've already betrayed him once for no real gain. Why not do it again for far more?"

"Dude, you don't have a clue. I've never felt like I was in Conryu's shadow and betraying him was the worst thing I've ever done. I'm just starting to earn his trust back. You think I'm going to throw it away for some bullshit promise from a demon?"

Asterion took another step. "You fear him. You fear that if you embrace your destiny as a hellpriest, Conryu will kill you. He may try, but my master is the strongest of the nine. With his might backing you up, even the Reaper's Chosen will fall."

"Spoken like someone that's never seen Conryu fight. Let me say this one more time. I ain't interested."

Jonny blinked and found Asterion standing right beside him. He had Lala by the neck and his feet were a foot off the ground.

"Let's try a different direction. Pledge yourself to the Horned One or your friend dies."

"Why are you so desperate for me to join your team?" Jonny asked. "Any of the psychos you brought in here to kill each other would've jumped at the chance to sell their souls for power."

"You have proven yourself adaptable, intelligent, and reasonably knowledgeable about how magic works. Your excessive morality is a problem, but one easily overcome once your soul has been corrupted." Asterion tightened his grip on Lala's throat, drawing a pained gurgle. "We're done talking. Pledge your soul or your friend dies and then you join him."

Jonny was about to tell him where he could shove his threats when a tremor ran through the arena. The floor shook with such force that the sand was bouncing. Cracks ran through the walls.

"Earthquake!" Jonny shouted. "Let's get out of here!"

"This is no earthquake." Asterion tossed Lala aside and turned to face a particular section of wall.

A moment later it collapsed and blinding sunlight shone through. A single figure stood in the opening outlined by the light.

"Do you have any idea how much trouble I had finding you?"

Jonny nearly collapsed with relief. Conryu was here. Thank heaven.

24

Conryu hovered above Crete, phone in hand, the map Maria had emailed him open on the screen. The quarry where they'd dealt with the fake temple had a little red X through it. An archeological site about fifty miles north and a partially restored ruin twenty miles east were the other spots she suggested as likely targets. Or at least the books she'd read on the subject suggested as much. Given the time span involved, it was all guesswork anyway.

He shrugged, might as well try the ruin first.

"I suggest the more distant target," Prime said.

"Why?"

"If the false temple we found was designed to act as a decoy, then it is most likely that the real temple would be as far away as possible."

"That works for me."

Conryu gathered power and launched himself north at about five hundred miles an hour. Only the light magic barrier that surrounded him made the pace tolerable. Another wizard would've had their face stretched out of shape from the friction. Not that many other wizards, even wind aligned ones, could get this sort of speed. In fact, he was pretty sure that Dean Blane was the only other wizard that even came close to matching him.

Soon enough they were flying over a grid of dug-up dirt. There was no sign of whoever was working the site, thank goodness. He spun in a slow circle and couldn't even see a village from here. It was the perfect spot to have a battle.

"Or to hide a temple," Prime said.

"Let's find out."

Conryu summoned his staff and a pulse of light magic shot out. Almost immediately it hit something. Something big.

"That's not an anchor point. It feels more like the entire temple."

"Even if it was invisible, anyone trying to walk through the space it occupied would run into the building." Prime swung left and right in his version of shaking his head. "This is something else."

"Such as?"

"My best guess is that the temple has been moved slightly out of phase with the real world. It's a variation on a pocket dimension. On the plus side, I believe you'll have an easier time gaining access. You just need to shift it back to our reality."

"Brilliant. How do I do that?"

"The same way you do everything, apply massive amounts of dark magic to the concealing spell until it shatters."

Conryu frowned, moderately annoyed. Was he really that predictable? After a moment's thought he was forced to admit that he was.

Oh, well. If it ain't broke, don't fix it.

He landed right beside the hidden temple and leveled the staff. The crystal on the end turned black and even the pleasant sunshine seemed to dim as power gathered. When he'd mustered every drop of power he could handle, Conryu released it in one shot.

Gray lines appeared in midair. It looked like the air was shattering.

The cracks quickly spread, revealing a Greek-style temple with white marble columns and a domed roof. It would've looked right at home in the acropolis.

Well, maybe not. It was in too good a shape.

Conryu grinned and pointed the staff again. He'd fix that in short order.

Earth magic crashed into the wall, shaking the entire temple, and sending a fair-sized section crumbling to the earth.

Inside, the temple looked like an arena, complete with a sand floor and seats full of spectators. Jonny stood staring at the hole Conryu had opened. A few feet from him a man in a black suit glared at Conryu. Dark magic, different from what Conryu wielded, seethed around him. A little further in, another fellow holding a pistol stood over a collapsed figure. They both looked like ordinary humans. A second man in black—Conryu recognized Cadus from Big Bob's memory—and a pair of bikini-clad women were far from ordinary judging by the corruption around them. A huge crowd of people filled the stands.

"The man in black is a demon, not a human," Prime said. "The temple's guardian demon, I'm certain. The other three appear to be lesser demons. The crowd is made up of demonic spirits."

"Excellent, that means we found the right place." Conryu turned to Jonny. "Do you have any idea how much trouble I had finding you?"

He strode through the opening he'd made. Trying to stay completely nonchalant, Conryu whispered, "Kai, as soon as I hit the demon, get Jonny out of here."

The guardian demon squared up in front of Conryu. "You've come a long way to die, Reaper's Chosen."

"I'm two and oh against guardian demons so far. What makes you think you'll fare any better?"

"Unlike those other fools, I'm not alone. Kill him!"

The spectators morphed from humans to demons and surged out of the seats.

A bullet pinged off his shield as the guy with the gun opened fire.

He only managed a single shot before one of Conryu's backup ninjas appeared and separated his head from his shoulders. Under the circumstances he didn't bother to criticize her for using excessive force.

The rest of the team appeared, cutting down demons as they flashed in and out of the borderland.

Kai had picked well. These ladies were clearly a cut above some of the others he'd seen.

Conryu sent a blast of divine white flames into the guardian demon, blowing him across the arena and slamming him into the wall. "Now, Kai."

Trusting his always-reliable partner to get Jonny out safe and sound, Conryu advanced on the guardian demon. The monster had already regained his feet. The front of his suit had been burned off, revealing the golden skin beneath. And that wasn't just the tone. It literally looked like he was made of gold.

Conryu stalked forward, ready for the next round.

He barely managed three steps before Cadus, now elongated to nearly seven feet tall with arms hanging down to his ankles, came charging in.

He had courage at least.

Divine white flames took him square in the chest.

The blast reduced everything above his waist to ash.

Unfortunately, the distraction gave the guardian demon a chance to fully recover. Anything human about the creature was long gone. He now stood nearly eight feet tall, sported the head of a bull, and appeared to be made of solid gold.

"That's the demon's true form," Prime said.

Conryu glanced at his familiar. "No kidding. Can you sense the temple core?"

"No, the demon's power is acting like a smokescreen for every-thing else in the temple. Once you kill him, I should be able to find it."

Conryu hoped it would be that easy.

"Chosen." Kai appeared beside him, sword drawn and ready. "Your friend is safe."

"Outstanding. What do you say we kill this thing?"

"I am with you, Chosen."

Conryu grinned. Hearing her say that always filled him with confidence.

"Master, watch out."

A ball of black energy had gathered between the demon's horns.

Conryu thrust the staff at it and loosed a sphere of dark magic.

The incompatible magics twisted and writhed. The demon howled and tossed its head from side to side as if trying to shake the darkness out.

When it succeeded, the corrupt energy smashed into the temple wall and melted another opening.

"Keep those things off me, Kai. I'm going to have to go all in to beat this monster."

"Nothing will touch you while I live."

Conryu summoned the white flames and merged his mind with them. The mingled power of fire and light plowed into the demon. Conryu was aware of nothing save the battle between divine flames and corruption.

The demon fought hard, maybe harder than any he'd battled so far, but inch by inch the white flames did their work.

And then it was gone.

He released the spell and looked around. The battle was over and the ninjas were standing around, swords drawn, alert for any other threats. Demon corpses slowly melted into black goo that sank into the sand.

"Where'd it go, Prime?"

"I caught a flash of movement as it fled down the tunnel. It's still in the temple somewhere. Probably gone to retrieve the temple core."

"Shit! The hunt isn't over then. And we don't dare let it escape. If it does, the damn thing will just start over somewhere else. Can the demon teleport without a powerful connection to its master's hell?"

"I hesitate to say given how little I know about this particular demon's abilities. It would certainly be within the realm of possibilities."

"Then we need a barrier. Something to keep it sealed inside."

"That I can help you with," Prime said. "But we'll need more ninjas for it to work."

"How many?" Conryu waved his reinforcements over.

"One every thirty feet around the temple. Their black iron swords will serve as the focus for the ritual."

He had no idea how big the temple was. Better to bring in all the help he could get.

The twelve ninjas joined him and bowed as one. None of them looked injured which confirmed his first thought that they were elite members of the group.

"You all did a fantastic job, thank you."

"They were weak," one of the ninjas said. "Do you need help hunting down the one that escaped?"

"Yes, but not in the way you mean. I want you to go back to the monastery and get everyone not currently on a mission. We're going to create a barrier to keep the demon from escaping. And hurry. I don't know how long we have."

They all vanished, leaving Conryu, Prime, and Kai alone surrounded by the dead.

"Chosen."

When Kai spoke, he turned to find Jonny making his hesitant way closer. Perfect. Jonny had been here for a while; he'd know what was down that tunnel.

"Prime, keep your senses sharp. If you detect any magic gathering, let me know and I'll blast it."

Jonny reached them, hesitated, and held out his fist. Conryu gave it a bump and he seemed to relax.

"Dude, am I glad to see you. I thought Asterion and his monsters were going to kill us all. If I ever volunteer to go undercover again, remind me of this."

"Who's Asterion?"

"The guy that turned into the golden bull thing. He seemed to be in charge."

"He's the temple's guardian demon, so that definitely makes him the one in charge. What's down that tunnel?" Conryu nodded toward the exit Asterion fled through.

"That's the living quarters. There's a dorm, a cafeteria, and a gym. Why would he go that way? It's not like there's anywhere to hide."

"I suspect there might be more than meets the eye. Thanks. I'm going to need you to wait outside."

"With pleasure. When you get a sec, my friend got pretty messed up during the fighting. Could you give him a look-see?"

Conryu frowned. "You got to be friends with one of the fighters?"

"Yeah, it's complicated."

Something shifted and Conryu found he was surrounded by nearly a hundred ninjas, with Kanna front and center.

"Let me get this sorted and we'll see. Prime, download the ritual into my head." He winced as the information was dumped into his brain. There had to be a more pleasant way of doing that.

"What are your orders, Chosen?" Kanna asked when he got closer.

"You guys are going to serve as the focus of a ritual to keep the guardian demon from escaping. I need you to space everyone thirty feet apart so you're completely—"

"Master!"

Conryu felt the power gathering an instant after Prime spoke. Dark magic lashed out, blowing the power source to bits.

Whether it was an attack or an escape attempt, Conryu didn't know, but he wasn't going to take a chance either way.

"Sorry. As I was saying, once you've got the temple surrounded, draw your swords and I'll use them as an anchor for a spell circle that will prevent the demon from escaping. Your magic will serve to maintain the spell, so I need you all to stay strong. I'd handle that part as well, but I'm going to need all the magic I can muster to bring down the demon and destroy the temple core."

"Have no fear, Chosen," Kanna said. "The demon will not escape while even one of us draws breath. Disperse!"

The ninjas vanished only to reappear outside a moment later. They had two ninjas along with Kai and Kanna to spare. Good thing he'd summoned everyone.

"Check them over, pal, make sure the spacing is right." Prime flew off to take a look and Conryu turned to Kanna. "I know you want to help me kill the demon, but I'm going to need you to stay here and maintain the circle. You have the strongest dark magic output which means I'm going to make you the core of the ritual."

Kanna's mask shifted and he suspected she was frowning under it. "As you command, Chosen."

He put a hand on her shoulder and leaned in to whisper, "I know I've given you some orders you haven't liked recently and I'm sorry, but this is where you can help the most. I'll be counting on you."

"I apologize, Chosen, for my lack of discipline. Grandmaster Narumi would be disgusted with my recent behavior. If this is where you need me, I will not let you down."

He gave her arm a final squeeze. "I have no doubt about that."

Prime came swooping out of the sky like the ugliest bird in history. "They're set, Master."

"Good." Conryu spotted the ninja that had spoken earlier, the one from the backup team. "Kanna, you'll be taking this young lady's place. Her skills impressed me earlier, so she'll be joining Kai and me when we make our move."

Kanna shot the woman a stern glare as she took her place. "You will be fighting at the Chosen's side, Tamaki. Bring honor to the Daughters of the Reaper."

Tamaki bowed. "I will not disappoint you, Grandmaster. It is an honor to fight with you, Chosen."

Conryu shifted his gaze to the other spare ninjas. "You two are on reserve. I don't think there are any dangers in the area, but your job is to protect your helpless sisters. I'm counting on you both to keep them safe."

Both women bowed.

He was as ready as he'd ever be.

"Draw swords!" His magnified voice shook the air.

As one the ninjas drew their weapons and held them up.

Now for the tricky part. Drawing on the knowledge Prime had fed him, Conryu shaped the spell circle, weaving it through the black iron, and creating a barrier impenetrable to magic.

When he was finished he nodded once, satisfied with what he'd created.

Now the clock was running. Time to kill the demon before it hit zero.

25

Conryu hurried across the sand of the arena with Kai and Tamaki at his side. The ritual that prevented the demon from escaping unfortunately kept them from shifting to the borderland. That might be a problem given how much their fighting style depended on being able to use that technique at will. But there was no help for it. He'd have to hope they could adapt.

The darkness beyond the tunnel entrance was absolute and his darkvision spell did nothing to penetrate it. Conryu raised his staff and white light burst from the crystal, pushing the darkness back. It felt like something was fighting him, trying to snuff out the light.

"That's probably the guardian demon," Prime said. "It's connected to everything in the temple. Its magic is powering the enchanted darkness."

Conryu swallowed a sigh. It was what it was. As always he'd deal with whatever he had to.

"Stay sharp. I can't get a read on anything beyond the light."

"Yes, Chosen," Tamaki and Kai said in unison.

He knew he didn't have to give them the warning, but he did it anyway. Better to be too careful than not careful enough.

The group descended the ramp with Conryu in the lead, the staff held high so the crystal was near the ceiling. The walls were made of gray stone and no seams were visible. The passage seemed to extend beyond the temple's wall. No doubt some other magic trick was responsible for that. Something like how he could make the library any size he wanted.

They finally reached the back wall and found a t-intersection. Nothing indicated the proper direction. Just once he'd like to find a sign with a big arrow that said "this way to the demon." Just for the novelty of it. If he ever did see such a thing it would obviously be a trap.

"Anybody good at mazes?"

No one spoke because of course they didn't. He was in charge. The decision was his.

Sometimes being in charge sucked.

He shrugged and turned right. As far as he could tell, one direction was as good as another in this place.

They had barely gone ten steps when Tamaki grabbed the back of his shirt. "There's a pressure plate just ahead, Chosen."

He stopped and frowned at the floor. The gray stone looked pretty much the same to him.

"Where?"

She pointed to a spot at the edge of the light. He squinted. "You mean that vague outline of a square? I wouldn't have even seen it."

He leveled the staff and loosed a burst of telekinesis to trigger the plate.

Black spikes shot out from the walls, ceiling, and floor. Whoever stepped on that would've had a really bad day.

"Hell-forged black iron," Prime said. "Your basic defensive spells might not have been enough to stop them."

"That's a cheery thought. Gold star to Tamaki for spotting the trigger. Why don't you take point? Clearly you've got a better eye for traps than I do."

"As you command, Chosen." Tamaki moved a couple strides ahead of him and they got moving again.

From behind Kai said, "Apologies for missing the pressure plate, Chosen."

"No worries, Kai. We're a team and not everyone can be the best at everything. It's not like I saw it either."

With Tamaki in the lead, they made good time, avoiding several more nasty traps along the way. While the traps were a pain, he fully expected to have to fight a bunch of demons as well. It would be a lucky break if they were all melting into puddles upstairs, but he refused to get his hopes up.

"There's a concentration of corruption a little way ahead, Master," Prime said. "I believe it's the guardian demon."

"Finally."

They rounded a corner and stepped through an arch into what looked like a duplicate of the arena upstairs. The only difference was, this one had an altar in the center with a crimson gem floating above it.

Asterion stood behind the altar flanked by a pair of minotaur demons nearly as tall as he was. Three on three, that was better odds than he feared.

When they were a few paces into the arena, a stone slab fell from the ceiling, blocking the exit. Looked like there was only one way out, and that was killing Asterion.

"You are a fool for coming here, Reaper's Chosen," Asterion said. "In this place my power is at its greatest. I will consecrate the temple with your life."

Conryu shook his head. "You're a hellpriest short for that to work. I know a bit about the rules of this game and only a hellpriest can consecrate a temple. You're just a guardian demon. Little more than a junkyard dog barking and tugging at his chain."

Asterion bared surprisingly sharp teeth for a bull's head. "Then I'll just kill you."

The lesser demons roared and charged.

"Those two are yours. Asterion is mine."

Conryu trusted Kai and Tamaki to handle the demons.

He sprinted forward, a bit of wind magic propelling him at near-blinding speed.

Divine white flames gathered around the tip of his staff.

He reached Asterion and swung hard.

Whether taken by surprise due to his speed or just overconfident, Asterion took the blow flush on the side of his head.

Light magic exploded out, sending him flying back into the rear wall of the arena. Asterion hit with enough force to crack the wall.

Having absolutely no desire to let him recover, Conryu sent a torrent of white flames roaring in.

The spell hit a barrier of corruption, just like last time.

The only hope he had of winning was to merge his mind with the flames and trust that Kai and Tamaki would keep the lesser demons from reaching him.

A moment later he became one with the flames.

———

Kai broke left, sword at the ready. A faint breeze ruffled her uniform as the Chosen raced ahead of them. The demon took a stride to follow him.

A slash from Kai's sword opened up its side and drew its attention to her. The wound didn't bleed and if the demon felt any pain, she couldn't tell. It bared its fangs, eyes glowing bloodred.

"That's right, demon, I'm your opponent. Forget that at your peril."

Whether incapable of speech or just uninterested, the demon charged, horns lowered to impale her.

Normally, Kai would've vanished into the borderland to avoid the attack. But that option had been denied her.

Instead she leapt right, rolled to her feet and slashed it again as it passed.

Her sword opened another slice in its golden flesh. Like the first it neither bled nor fazed the monster.

The sounds of Tamaki's battle and the roar of the Chosen's flames filled the air. How many of these fights had she been in since joining him what seemed a lifetime 'ago? Kai couldn't remember, but many.

The demon finally brought itself around to face her. It didn't seem especially clever as such things went, but its strength and durability couldn't be denied. She needed a plan if she wanted to kill it.

It roared, but didn't charge this time. The creature stalked closer, massive fists raised.

"So you can learn. I had my doubts at first."

She moved forward to meet it, sword at middle guard.

Kai blinked and the demon closed the distance between them in an instant.

An instinctive block saved her from a right fist that would've caved in her chest.

The blow sent her flying halfway across the arena.

Her hands vibrated from the power of the blow. At least her sword appeared unharmed. Such was the strength of Hell-forged black iron.

The demon seemed determined to press its advantage.

It closed the distance between them again, raining blows that she dodged by the narrowest of margins. Having seen what would happen, Kai wouldn't try and block unless she had no other choice.

Its left fist missed her chin by a hair.

Kai countered, slashing hard at its shoulder.

A deep gash opened, but she didn't sever its arm as she'd hoped.

A backhand blow from the same arm knocked the air out of her and sent her flying a second time.

The wound must have weakened it. This time it only sent her a quarter of the way across the arena.

Instead of attacking, it turned to face the defenseless Chosen.

A black sphere formed between its horns.

She struggled to her feet, gasping for breath.

Kai had to reach the demon in time. She couldn't let Conryu die.

Tamaki got there first.

A slice from her sword severed one horn. The dark magic the demon had been gathering dissipated.

Tamaki kept up her assault, slashing high and low, opening numerous wounds on the monster before driving her sword up to the hilt in its chest.

The demon slumped to its knees.

Tamaki ripped her sword free and hacked the monster's head off for good measure.

Kai finally made it to her feet and glanced right to see the second demon slowly rotting into the sand. Some bodyguard she was.

Tamaki flicked the ichor off her sword and sheathed it. "Are you hurt, sister?"

Kai shook her head. "Just a few bruises. Many thanks for the timely assistance."

"We all serve him to the best of our ability."

Both women turned to watch the final battle. The white flames were blinding and Kai couldn't tell who was winning. At least her eyes couldn't. Her heart knew for sure that Conryu would come out on top.

———

Conryu gathered every drop of magic he could muster, focused his will, and sent it all against Asterion. The guardian demon resisted with such ferocity that it felt like trying to melt steel with a cigarette lighter. The first temple guardian he'd fought put up a hell of a fight too, but nothing compared to this. How could there be such a difference in their power levels?

Asterion took a step forward, actually pushing through the torrent of flames. He felt the demon's corruption burning away moment by moment, but it generated more so quickly his spell couldn't reach the monster's golden skin.

As soon as the thought crossed his mind, Conryu knew what he was doing wrong.

Shifting the spell's focus, he narrowed the blast into a lance focused on a spot about two inches in diameter. The white lance drilled through the demon's barrier in an instant, burning a perfect circle through its chest.

Asterion howled in pain.

Conryu's expression remained grim as he sent a second lance racing out.

Asterion tried to dodge, but he caught the demon in the side, burning a gouge across its ribs.

This wasn't as efficient a way to fight, but at least it worked.

Beam after beam shot out, some missing but more hitting. Soon the demon looked like a Swiss-cheese statue rather than a golden one. Unfortunately the many holes in its torso did little to slow it down.

Even worse, Conryu was feeling the effects of so much prolonged magic use. He wasn't that close to backlash yet, but if he didn't end this fight soon he would be.

Time to try another trick.

He sent a lance out and when Asterion tried to dodge, commanded it to change course. The beam of white energy bent, taking the demon in the right knee and burning his lower leg off.

Asterion crashed to the floor.

This was his chance.

Multiple beams shot out, driving into the holes he already made then expanding and burning Asterion from the inside out.

He was weakening now.

Conryu poured in every drop of magic he could muster.

White flames shot out of Asterion's eyes and mouth.

With a final flash the demon was fully consumed.

Conryu dropped to his knees, panting for breath.

"Chosen!" Kai appeared at his side. "Are you okay?"

"More or less. That was tough. This thing made the vine demon we fought look like a real pushover. In my wildest dreams I didn't imagine something resisting the divine white flames like that. Maybe the Horned One really is the strongest of the demon lords."

"No, Master," Prime said. "It's not that the Horned One is stronger. All the demon lords are omnipotent within their hells. The problem is that this is the strongest temple you've fought in. When the lesser demons were slain earlier, their corruption was added to the temple's, making it and the guardian stronger. It's a clever bit of magic, I've never seen anything like it before."

Conryu forced himself to his feet. "And you didn't think to mention any of this earlier?"

"I didn't realize it earlier. While you all were busy fighting, I studied the magic. A closer examination made it clear that the aura of corruption was stronger now than when we arrived."

"Great. Let's deal with the temple core. Purifying the rest will keep until later."

"It'll be easier for you if you take the core outside," Prime said.

"I'm all for that. We need to tell Kanna she can release the ritual as well."

"I'll carry the core for you, Chosen." Tamaki reached for the crystal.

Before her hands could make contact, Conryu thrust the staff out, blocking her way. "The demon's essence is still inside. You really don't want to touch it barehanded."

Tamaki drew back as if scalded. "Apologies, Chosen."

"No need for that." Conryu made a little circle above the core and a light magic barrier formed around it. "There, now it's safe to handle. I'd appreciate it if you carried the cursed thing for me. Kai, I might need a shoulder to lean on, so stay close."

"I have you, Chosen, don't fear."

"On the plus side," Prime said. "We shouldn't have to worry about traps on the way out."

Everyone looked at him and Prime somehow managed to look sheepish. A remarkable feat for a demon book.

The trio set out, Tamaki a little bit ahead of Conryu and Kai. The staff had been reduced to little more than a crutch for the moment and Kai looked like she feared he might fall flat on his face. Not at all an unreasonable concern.

"You two did good handling those minotaur demons."

Kai looked away. "Tamaki defeated them both, saving you in the process. I was of little help."

"I'm sure you did fine." Conryu straightened a little as his strength slowly returned.

"No, I didn't. Her skills are far more refined than mine. Having seen that, I wonder if it would be better for Tamaki to take my place as your bodyguard."

"Forget that. After everything we've been through, there's no way someone's taking your place. I have total faith that you can handle anything you need to. That said, whenever we need backup, Tamaki's going to the top of my contact list."

"I appreciate your confidence in me, Chosen, though I'm uncertain I'm worthy of it."

He reached out, took her hand, and gave it a little squeeze, trying to convey as much reassurance as he could. "You and me, no matter what. Right?"

"Until the Reaper calls me to Black City, my sword is yours, unworthy though it might be."

Conryu gave a little shake of his head. Maybe Kanna would have some idea about how to help her get her confidence back. He was too exhausted to think about it right now.

Prime turned out to be correct about the lack of traps and they made good time back to the exit. A wave of his staff ended the barrier. Up and down the line, ninjas sat down before they fell down. He'd never seen the usually indomitable women look so tired. Only Kanna remained on her feet.

He walked over to her, trying to project more strength than he felt. "Great work keeping the barrier up."

"It was more difficult than I expected, Chosen, but everyone did their best. Is it over?"

"No, but the immediate threat is dealt with. I still need to destroy the temple core and purify the rest of the structure, but the guardian demon has been slain and its essence returned to the core. For now, let's get you all back to the monastery for a well-deserved rest."

"I don't think anyone is strong enough to shift to the border-land," Kanna said.

"No worries." Conryu summoned the library door and opened it. "Could you get everyone inside? I need to call Maria."

Kanna bowed and started rounding up her people.

"What should I do with this, Chosen?" Tamaki held up the core.

"Hang on to it for now. I'll deal with it once I regain my strength. Make sure no one else touches it, and I mean no one. Okay?"

"As you command, Chosen."

Conryu had his phone halfway out of his pocket when Jonny came jogging over.

"Dude, you look like shit. Everything okay?"

Conryu smiled. "Things are as good as can be expected. I've still got a bunch of cleanup work to do, but Asterion is dead and his spirit has returned to the temple core. Without him causing trouble, the temple isn't much of a threat. And I didn't forget about your friend, I just need a rest before I heal him."

"Thanks. Lala might be a bit of a homicidal maniac, but he's still one of the nicer people I've met."

"If that's true, then you seriously need to get out of the Department more often, but not undercover."

Jonny grinned. "Amen to that."

"You guys can load up with the ninjas. I'll be along in a minute." They bumped fists and Jonny hurried back the way he'd come to collect his friend.

"You're too easy on him," Kai said. "He betrayed you once, he might do so again."

"You might be right, but we've been friends a long time. If anyone deserves a second chance, Jonny does."

He brought up Maria's number and hit dial.

She picked up after one ring. "Are you okay? Did you find Jonny?"

"Yes to both. I'm tired but uninjured and Jonny is fine. Also, I need a favor."

"If it's within my power, just name it."

"The temple ended up being at the site of an archeological dig. I need you to make arrangements with the authorities in Crete to keep everyone away from it until I have a chance to purify the corruption. I don't think it's actually dangerous, but that level of dark magic can't be good for your health long-term, assuming you're not a dark aligned wizard of course."

"That's a bit outside my authority, but I'll talk to Dad. I'm sure he knows someone."

"Thanks. I'm going to be out of touch for a little while, but don't worry, I'm just taking a rest. This was a tough one."

"Okay, but don't be a stranger. Love you."

"Love you too."

He hung up and started to pocket his phone when it rang.

Conryu checked the screen and frowned. What could Kelsie want?

"Hey, what's up?"

"I've got a problem and I really didn't want to bother you, but I don't know who else to call, I'm so sorry." The words all came out in a rush and she sounded on the verge of tears.

"Okay, take a breath and tell me about it."

After a minute, her voice steady, Kelsie told him about the break-in and the ensuing investigation. Now it seemed the investigator had gone missing which implied that the wizard involved was stronger than they first thought.

"Anyway, could you swing by the lab and make sure the team is okay and if they're not see what you can do about the thieves?"

Conryu held the phone away from his face, ran his fingers through his hair, and swallowed a scream. If Malice was in any way involved, she should've called him before sending her team in. Even dead and rotting in hell the evil old woman was causing him problems.

He frowned. She was rotting in hell, right? He needed to look into that.

"Give me an hour. I'll meet you at your place before heading to the lab."

"Thanks. And I really am sorry to be such a pain."

"Don't worry about it. But if you want to make it up to me, have that chef of yours fix me something delicious for when I get there. It's been about half a day since I ate anything and I'm starving."

"I can do that. What do you want?"

"Anything, as long as it's hot and filling."

"Okay, see you in an hour."

She disconnected and he pocketed his phone.

"More trouble, Chosen?" Kai asked. "An hour isn't long for you to recover."

"On the contrary, as long as we stay in the library, an hour can be a lifetime. Come on, let's get everyone home."

26

It took little more than the blink of an eye to move everyone from Crete to the monastery that served as the ninjas' base. Conryu opened the door and stepped out into the courtyard. Kai came immediately after him and took her place at his side. While he didn't know if she'd gotten her confidence back, she at least didn't look as depressed as she had earlier. That was a relief.

One after another, weary, staggering ninjas emerged from the library. Some of them looked okay and others looked like staying upright was taking all they had. He spotted Kanna and waved her over.

"You guys look done in. I'll send a message to Talon and ask him to have some of his people keep an eye out for trouble. I doubt there'll be issues, but until you all recover, better safe than sorry."

"Ordinarily I'd say there was no need for you to worry, Chosen, but in this case I humbly accept your suggestion." Kanna must have been tired if she wasn't even going to argue.

"I'd like to borrow Tamaki as well, at least until I've got this business with Kelsie sorted out."

Kanna chuckled. "We are always at your disposal, Chosen. You don't need to ask my permission to claim one of the Daughters anytime you need her."

"I know, but there's no need to be rude about it. Have a good rest. I'll see you in a while."

The last of the ninjas had exited the library along with Jonny and Lala. The bald fighter was limping and kind of hunched over. It wouldn't take much to heal him, so best to get that out of the way.

The staff's crystal turned white as he approached the pair and released a wave of healing magic.

Jonny let out a long sigh. "Thanks, dude. That never gets old."

Lala bounced around on his toes and did a little shadow boxing. "Yes, indeed. I haven't felt this good in years. If I may ask, where are we?"

"The Land of the Night Princes," Conryu said. "Don't worry, I'll drop you two off somewhere a bit more hospitable. Where do you want to go?"

"Central for me," Jonny said. "If possible, at the Department of Magic. I need to report in. I imagine the rest of the team is frantic."

"I let Maria know you were okay a little while ago, so I'm sure she's told her father by now. Still, I'm happy to leave you there." Conryu turned to Lala. "And you?"

Lala twirled his mustache as he thought. "I'm currently unemployed and without prospects. Central is fine for me as well. Finding a job shouldn't be difficult."

"You can crash at my place until you get settled," Jonny said.

"Very kind, my friend. I'm so glad I didn't end up having to kill you."

Conryu shook his head. "Jump back in the library. I'll be along in a sec."

"Chosen." Tamaki picked that moment to approach. She'd left the temple core in the library surrounded by his light magic barrier. It would be secure there until he had a chance to destroy it. "The grandmaster said you wished me to remain on standby for a little longer."

"Yes, please. I have no idea what we're dealing with and having an extra sword wouldn't hurt anything. You and Kai working together should be able to handle anything Malice's friend can throw at us."

"I am honored by your confidence," Tamaki said. "I'll wait in the borderland until you need me."

She bowed and vanished.

"You're cool with this, right?" Conryu asked Kai.

"Of course. If you're expecting trouble, having Tamaki with us is a prudent decision."

She said all the right things, but Conryu still couldn't decide if she meant them or not. And he didn't have time to worry about it either. After sending a psychic message to Talon, the pair joined Jonny and Lala in the library. It took only an instant to open the library door again, this time on the Department of Magic's parking lot.

"I didn't know magic of this sort existed," Lala said.

"It doesn't," Conryu said. "And if anyone asks, that's what you tell them."

"Ah, understood. Thank you for the ride."

"Later, bro," Jonny said.

Conryu nodded and closed the library door. He only shifted them from the parking lot to the garage across the street before opening the door again.

"I need to make a quick trip to Hell. I've got a bad feeling in the pit of my stomach. Hopefully the Reaper can reassure me that I'm wrong."

"You're going to speak to the master?" Kai said.

"Yeah, just a quick side trip. You don't have to come if you don't want to."

"No, I'll join you of course. I was just surprised."

Conryu opened a hell portal and stepped through to find Tamaki petting Cerberus. She immediately snapped to attention and moved away from him. "Forgive me, Chosen. I was just getting to know your guardian demon."

"That's no problem." Conryu patted Cerberus on the flank. "I'm glad to see you two getting along. I'm headed for Black City. Want to come?"

Tamaki shook her head. "I'll stay here on guard."

"Okay, we shouldn't be long."

He and Kai settled on Cerberus's back and then they were off like a rocket.

It seemed they hadn't been moving anytime when Black City appeared in the distance. Dimly lit by eerie red lights and constructed of black stone, the city was the capital of the Reaper's hell as well as the seat of his power. It could be as big or as small, as near or as far as the Reaper wished. It seemed today he wished it close and that suited Conryu fine. His whole body ached and he wanted nothing so much as a twelve-hour nap.

At the center of the city stood a massive black citadel complete with jutting towers, a wall, and black-winged angels on guard duty. Speaking of the former ninjas, one of them came soaring their way. As with all of them, she was a flawless beauty, with pale, perfect skin, a killer body, glowing red eyes, and black-feathered wings.

"Welcome, Chosen," she said. "Are you here to see the master?"

"Yeah, is he in a good mood?"

"Better than sometimes. Good luck with your audience."

She flew off and Cerberus landed in the courtyard. "You two better wait here. I won't be long."

Kai bowed. "If you insist, Chosen."

Conryu grinned. No one ever argued very hard when told they could avoid a meeting with Death.

The citadel doors, gigantic things made of solid black iron, opened at his approach. As soon as Conryu stepped through them he found himself in the Reaper's audience chamber. The big man himself sat on his throne. None of the demon lord's body was visible under his black robe and his scythe was resting against the throne's arm. The black-winged angels on guard duty stood at attention along the wall.

"What troubles you, my Chosen?" the Reaper asked.

"I have a really bad feeling and I was hoping you could confirm something for me. Did Malice Kincade's soul end up here somewhere?"

"No, Baphomet snatched her up before she reached me. Pity she died in his temple. Her corrupt soul would've done my hell some good."

"Shit! I was afraid of that. Thanks for the confirmation. I have to get back."

"Well done with the Horned One's temple by the way," the Reaper added before Conryu could leave. "And just to be clear, he is not stronger than me."

That last sentence sent a particularly powerful chill down Conryu's spine. "Never doubted that for a second. Until next time."

Conryu blinked and found himself back in the courtyard.

"I'm impressed, Master," Prime said. "You got both a compliment and a vague threat out of him in as many sentences.

"I could've done without the threat, but thanks."

"Chosen," Kai said as she and Cerberus walked up to him. "Is all well?"

"Not in the least, but what else is new? I need to visit the forge masters then we'll head back."

"Do you need a new weapon?"

"No, a gift."

27

Conryu settled on a ten-hour nap in the library and when he woke up he found his body rested and his magic restored. Best of all, he would still be early to meet Kelsie. Kai took the opportunity to sleep as well and he didn't even have to argue with her. It was a nice change of pace.

Before opening the door, he took a moment to check on the temple core. The light magic bubble looked unchanged, but he poured more power into it just to be safe. Without a body, the guardian demon shouldn't be able to affect anything, but if there was one thing he'd learned since the recent chaos began, it was not to take anything for granted.

He finally opened the library door directly in front of Kelsie's mansion. He could've gone right to wherever she was waiting—the Kincades' wards, powerful as they were, didn't pose much of a danger to him. But it seemed more polite to knock.

So he did.

A few seconds later a vulture-looking butler in a black suit opened the door and bowed to him. "You are expected, sir. Lady Kincade is waiting in the dining room. Follow me, please."

The inside of Kincade Manor looked just as he remembered,

big, cold, and impersonal. Clearly Kelsie hadn't had a chance to redecorate. Or maybe she wasn't going to bother. One set of ridiculously expensive decorations was pretty much the same as another.

Jeeves opened a door and there, seated at the head of a table big enough to hold fifty, was Kelsie. She was in her business outfit tonight, dark suit jacket, white blouse, and pencil skirt. It was a beautiful look. Pity the dark circles under her eyes ruined the effect.

She started to stand but he waved her back. "No need for formality between us. Though given the setting formality does seem appropriate. How are you holding up?"

"Stressed, but otherwise okay. It's been worse since the break-in."

"Sorry to hear it. Now I fear I'm going to have to add to your stress."

"That doesn't surprise me. Go ahead."

"Turns out, Malice's soul didn't end up in the Reaper's hell. Baphomet grabbed it first. From what you've told me plus what I've heard from other sources, my working theory is that one of your thieves is Miguel, Baphomet's hellpriest. And the second is Malice herself, now transformed into a demon."

Kelsie's mouth opened and closed but no words came out.

"I feel the same way. On the plus side, I've been looking for Miguel. Assuming this is him, it'll be the prefect chance to finish off another hellpriest."

A different door opened and when it did the smell of cooking meat wafted out. A female servant poked her head in. "Dinner's ready."

"Great, I'm starving. Kai, do you and Tamaki want something to eat?"

"We're good, Chosen, thank you." Kai's soft whisper made it sound like her lips were right beside his ear.

"Who's Tamaki?" Kelsie asked as the servant set a plate loaded with a two-inch-thick ribeye steak and fat, twice-cooked French fries in front of him.

"One of the ninjas. She's an awesome fighter and assuming my theory is correct, an extra sword will be welcome."

He dug into the food and sighed with the first bite. How long since he'd had steak? Too long was the obvious answer.

"This is delicious, thank you."

"Anytime." She hesitated a moment then said, "Is my grandmother alive?"

"Not in a human way," Prime said. "Her soul has been bonded with a demonic body, thus creating a semi-autonomous demon."

"How do you know?" Conryu asked around a mouthful of steak. "We haven't even seen her yet."

"That's how all demons capable of independent thought and action are created. The Dark Lady, even Cerberus and myself were created the same way. I can't imagine Baphomet uses a different process than the Reaper."

"If it's her soul controlling the demon body," Kelsie said. "That would explain how she knew so much about Kincade West and about the alchemy lab."

"Certainly," Prime said. "I have no doubt Baphomet chose her for exactly that reason."

"That's a relief," Kelsie said.

"Why?" Conryu asked.

"Because it likely means there isn't some faction loyal to her memory trying to undercut my authority. That was my biggest worry."

Conryu cocked his head. "Really? I'm more worried about what Demon Malice and her master are planning in a giant alchemy lab. What exactly is the lab used for?"

Kelsie's cheeks had reddened and she said, "I'm worried about that too. The lab was used to create homunculi, artificial life forces like our head butler. The cost proved prohibitive, so he was the only one ever made. The place has been mothballed for a decade."

"Why not clean it out and make sure it couldn't be used again?" Conryu asked.

"You'd have to ask Mother and Grandmother about that. I didn't even know it existed until a few weeks ago."

Conryu placed his knife and fork on his now-empty plate. "Time to get back to work. Just to clarify, it's okay if I level this place during the fight, right?"

"That might be for the best. The lab would be removed as a threat and I can collect the insurance."

Conryu grinned and pushed away from the table. "Sounds like a win-win to me. So what's the address?"

When she told him Conryu said, "I've never visited that part of Central."

"You're not missing anything. Good luck and maybe come by again when there isn't a world-threatening danger waiting for dessert."

"I'd like that. Later." He opened a hell portal and stepped through. Now it was time to see what the old hag was up to.

———

M iguel stood in front of one of the cylinders and stared at the creature inside. Despite how human they looked, he refused to call the unnatural things people. Not that he was one to talk. Given his current circumstance, Miguel wasn't sure whether he qualified as human either.

Speaking of unnatural creatures, he flicked a glance at Malice. She'd been sitting and brooding for hours. Clearly her failure to find whatever it was she'd been looking for was weighing on her mind. He considered, briefly, very briefly, asking if she wanted to talk or if there was anything he could do to help. However, nothing about her behavior or posture suggested that she wanted company or input. Better to wait until she asked him.

He turned back to the cylinder and found the thing inside staring at him. "Gah!"

He staggered back, eager to put as much distance as possible between him and the creature. They were unpleasant enough to look at with their eyes closed. Having them look back was just disgusting.

"Can't you keep quiet and sit still for ten minutes?" Malice asked.

"Sorry." Miguel didn't know why he was apologizing. Maybe it was because when she spoke in that tone Malice reminded him of his late grandmother. "One of those things opened its eyes and looked at me. I was startled for a moment."

"Excellent." Malice climbed to her feet. "If their eyes are open, it means the process is nearly complete."

She walked over to the nearest ethereal generator and gave it a close look. After a moment of study she nodded and moved on to the next one and the next.

When she'd checked them all she said, "Five more minutes. I didn't bother with a personality implant since they'll just be serving as hosts for demonic spirits. We can begin the transformation as soon as they're fully formed."

"You said you wanted me to summon the strongest spirits I could, right?"

"Yes, for the first batch at least. As soon as we're done with them, we can sacrifice the prisoners to summon a Black Eternal. That will make enhancing the second batch much easier."

Miguel nodded, a little smile curling his lips. Finally, his new army was about to begin taking shape.

Five minutes felt like five hours but at last the ethereal sparks stopped shooting out of the generators. Malice raised her hands and the creatures slowly rose up and out of the tanks. Though they looked like men, they were sexless and hairless. Perhaps fleshy mannequins would be a better description.

When their feet hit the floor they straightened and stared at nothing in particular. Miguel shuddered, once again reminded of how inhuman the things were.

"They're ready to receive the demon spirits," Malice said.

Right, he didn't have time to be fooling around. Miguel took a deep breath and drew on his connection to Baphomet. A swirling black portal about two feet across opened. At his mental command, four humanoid shadows emerged and flew into the bodies waiting for them.

The mannequins twitched and shuddered as the demon spirits settled into place.

Miguel finally had to look away. The process was just too much for him. He felt like a weakling for doing it, but he'd feel even worse if he threw up. Assuming he could throw up. He hadn't actually eaten anything in days.

"It's done," Malice said, glee in her voice.

He turned back to find the thralls standing at attention, their eyes glowing like embers. The corruption surrounding them was darker and thicker than any thrall he'd ever created before. That had to be a good sign.

"You did well," Malice said. "They'll make fine troops."

Was that the first compliment she'd given him? It felt like it.

"Should we begin summoning the Black Eternal?"

She had her head cocked like she was listening to something he couldn't hear.

Miguel sensed it a moment later, a powerful, dark presence. One he'd felt once before.

"He's here," Malice said. "It seems our troops are going to get tested sooner than we'd hoped."

Miguel bared his teeth. The Reaper's Chosen had arrived. This time would be different. This time, Miguel would be the one to emerge victorious.

28

Conryu had visited some sketchy places over the years, but the neighborhood surrounding the Kincade warehouse had to be one of the rougher ones. In fact, it wouldn't have looked out of place as a suburb of Black City.

He emerged from the hell portal around dusk. Though it was probably a waste of effort, he'd chosen to appear beside the security team's armored truck about half a block from the warehouse. Approaching on foot was a basic, and likely unnecessary, precaution. Still, better safe than sorry.

A broken sidewalk ran all the way to a chain-link fence that surrounded a large, industrial warehouse. It was the best-looking building in the area, which wasn't saying much. The gate was already open and a sleek sedan was parked in front of it. That it hadn't been completely stripped for parts seemed something of a minor miracle.

He cocked his head.

"Master."

"I sense it too, pal. This is definitely the right place. And that's a whole heap of corruption. I hope they haven't killed Kelsie's employees yet. She's likely to blame herself if anything happens to them."

Conryu took a moment to strengthen his defenses and shared the spells with Prime. Ready as he'd ever be, he marched towards the warehouse, every sense alert for danger.

To his surprise, he didn't encounter a single ward and the side door appeared unprotected as well. Just to be safe, he poked it open with the staff. The door swung open with a faint squeak, revealing rows of barrels sitting on pallets. If not for the corruption under his feet seething like magma in a volcano waiting to erupt, he'd be inclined to think this was nothing more than an ordinary warehouse.

Now, Kelsie said there was supposed to be an elevator in the center of the building.

Ten strides in, the floor exploded as vines shot up like tentacles, trying to wrap around him.

His light magic barrier reduced them to ash.

With a thought wind magic lifted him safely up and away from the crumbling floor. Through the hole he spotted a mad scientist's lab complete with what looked like four monsters. Those had to be the homunculi. All four of the naked figures looked up at him with burning red eyes.

Miguel and Malice stood off to one side. Both looked exactly as he remembered, including Miguel's hate-twisted face. Malice's expression showed nothing of her feelings, but her glowing red eyes confirmed her demonic nature.

Miguel pointed and more vines appeared out of nowhere only to meet the same fate as the first batch.

"Keep your distance, Prime." Though he didn't speak, Conryu sensed his familiar's confirmation. "Kai, Tamaki, find the security team and get them to safety."

Orders given, he descended to the lab floor.

"You will not defeat me this time!" Miguel said.

Conryu cocked an eyebrow. "Given our previous encounter, what makes you believe that?"

"This time I have powerful allies and you are alone."

"One of your allies is well known to me. Pity you didn't stay dead, Malice."

"Despite your best efforts, you mean," she spat back at him.

"No more talk. Kill him!" At Miguel's command, the four possessed homunculi sprang forward.

"You made one serious mistake." A heaven portal appeared beside Conryu. "I'm not alone. To battle!"

A squad of elves sprinted out of the portal, led by his father. Their silvery swords gleamed in the light.

Vines shot out, trying to wrap them up.

Razor-sharp mithril blades turned the vines into salad in an instant.

The monsters did a little bit better. Their speed allowed them to avoid a few slashes, but they were forced to back up inch by inch. It was only a matter of time before they ran out of room to run.

Conryu trusted the elves to deal with those things. He turned his focus on Malice and Miguel. With the portal draining his strength, a full-power blast of divine white flames was out of the question. But he did have a new trick he wanted to try.

Leveling the staff at Malice, he wrapped the evil old woman in alternating bands of light and dark magic, making sure the opposing magics never made contact.

She snarled and tried to break out.

As soon as her flesh made contact with the light magic band she jerked it back. A section of her skin had been burned away.

Conryu grinned. The binding magic worked just as he'd hoped. He shifted his gaze to Miguel, eager to give the hellpriest a taste of the same.

His smile withered as vines wrapped around the young man and he vanished to heaven alone knew where. The son of a bitch might not be able to travel through his master's hell the way Conryu could, but that trick with the vines was just as big of a problem.

Putting Miguel out of his mind for the moment, Conryu refocused on the elves' battle. He turned just in time to see the end of it as his father cut the last monster standing in half. Their task complete, the elves marched back through the gate. His father paused long enough to give Conryu a brief nod of acknowledgement. That little gesture was more than enough to remind him that, no matter what he looked like now, his father was still there.

The portal closed and he let out a long breath. That trick really took a toll.

Kai appeared and bowed. "The soldiers were still alive, though bound in vines. We freed them, but getting them out of this basement was more than we could manage."

"Great work, thanks."

He walked over to Malice, who glared daggers at him with her now-glowing red eyes. "I suppose you're going to kill me again."

Conryu shook his head. "No, I've got another plan in mind for you."

Her arrogant sneer vanished. "I insist that you kill me. Right this second."

"So you can be reborn in Baphomet's hell? I don't think so. Since Miguel got away, it wouldn't take him long to summon you back to cause me yet more trouble. No, I have something more permanent in mind."

"What are you going to do?" This was the first time he could remember hearing Malice sound nervous.

"Kai, keep an eye on the security officers. I need to make a quick trip to Black City."

"As you command, Chosen."

He walked over to Malice and opened a portal directly under them both.

K ai didn't know what Conryu was thinking and that always
bothered her. When he refused to kill Malice, she couldn't
have been more surprised. That horrid woman had been causing
him problems for as long as Kai had known him. On the other
hand, taking Malice to the master might well be a fate worse than
death.

With nothing better to do until he returned, she strode over to
the soldiers—no, security officers, that's what he called them,
though the difference between the two designations escaped her.

Halfway there Tamaki appeared beside her. "Did you know he
could summon mystical warriors to fight for him?"

"They were elves, but yes, I saw him summon the Heavenly
warriors once before. They are formidable, but maintaining their
presence in this world drains him a great deal."

"I would very much like to test myself against them. Their
speed and skill with a sword are truly terrifying."

"Once he's recovered, I'm sure the Chosen would be happy to
grant your wish. You should ask him."

Tamaki shook her head. "Given his many responsibilities, I
would not want to trouble him with my selfish request."

Kai very much respected Tamaki's attitude, but she still didn't
know Conryu well. Few things pleased him more than being able
to do something kind for others.

The pair reached the officers, who had gained their feet and
appeared little worse off for their rough treatment. One of them
stepped forward and offered a nod. "My team and I are much
obliged for the rescue, ma'am. My name is Artyom and I'm
guessing the young man that just left is Conryu Koda. Ms.
Kincade speaks very highly of him."

"Kelsie has been a great friend to the Chosen," Kai said. "He
will lift you out of here when he returns."

"That's fine, ma'am. We're not going anywhere. If it's okay, I would like to contact headquarters and let them know we're safe."

"That's fine, but don't summon anyone here. This building is scheduled for demolition."

Artyom's brow furrowed. "I'm not sure I understand."

"Kelsie told the Chosen that he should destroy the lab, warehouse and all. I believe she intends to say there was an accident and claim the insurance."

Artyom's lip curled in a faint smile. "That girl is more of a Kincade than I thought. I guess as long as it doesn't go beyond insurance fraud there's no problem. Excuse me."

He moved a few feet away and pulled out a cellphone that crumbled to bits.

Kai pointed to the far end of the lab. "I believe the phone on the wall is functional."

He went to make his call and Kai kept her distance to give him a bit of privacy. Conryu should be back any second, but she would remain in this reality to keep an eye on Artyom and his companions until he returned.

29

As soon as the boy's hell portal closed, Malice noticed a deep growling. The three-headed demon dog Cerberus padded closer, fangs bared and eyes glowing bright red. There were no other demons in the area; probably didn't want to end up devoured by the beast.

She shuddered. Was that what he had planned for her?

Conryu drifted over and patted Cerberus on the flank. "Now, now. She's a present for the boss demon himself. We can't have you chewing on her before she's delivered."

He was taking her to the Reaper? That sounded vastly worse than getting devoured.

"Why not just kill me and have it over with?"

"I already told you why. Satisfying as it would be to keep killing you over and over again, I've got too much to do. By the way, you're starting to dissolve."

She hardly needed him to tell her that. Her body was paralyzed, she couldn't access any of her magic, and the demonic essence that formed her body had begun to deteriorate. Hardly surprising given that she couldn't access any of Baphomet's power here.

"Since I don't want you reduced to a disembodied soul just yet, we'd best get a move on." He pointed and Malice floated up right in front of Cerberus's central head. "I'm going to need you to carry her, boy. Gently, please."

The demon dog growled at her, but when its massive jaws closed on her, it was as gentle as a mother cat carrying her kitten. Glad as she was not to be torn to shreds, getting carried into Black City like this had to be among the more embarrassing things Malice had ever experienced.

"Good boy, let's go."

And they were off like a shot. All Malice could see was the endless darkness and the grinning idiot riding on Cerberus's back. Since she'd been reborn in Baphomet's hell, Malice had wondered from time to time whether she would've been better off just accepting her fate and dying like a regular person. Depending on how things went with the Reaper, just dying might not be so bad.

Soon, too soon as far as she was concerned, the streets of Black City appeared below her. They didn't slow until Cerberus halted in the courtyard of a massive black fortress. Malice had never actually visited the Reaper in person. She used to have an agent here, but the bond shattered when she died.

Conryu hopped down and gestured. Cerberus let go and she floated down beside him. Her fingers had been reduced to half their length and both her feet were gone. At least slowly dissolving wasn't painful. That came as a surprise.

"Wait here, boy. I need to go talk to you-know-who."

Cerberus whined, displaying his considerable intelligence.

"Don't worry. We're all on the same team here. Well, not her, but you know what I mean. Now behave. I shouldn't be long."

Cerberus plopped down on his haunches and panted. Seeing an eight-foot-tall, three-headed dog acting like a family pet had to be among the stranger sights she'd seen. And that was saying something.

"What exactly are you planning to do with me?" Malice asked as she floated along behind him to the citadel gates. She hated the fear in her voice.

"I don't want to spoil the surprise."

"I'm supposed to be the evil one, not you."

He just grinned that arrogant, infuriating grin and pushed the doors open. One stride found them in the Reaper's throne room. The demon lord sat upon his throne, but it was the huge glass cylinder that looked like it was filled with fireflies that caught Malice's attention. That held all the souls that had pledged themselves to the Reaper but that he hadn't gotten around to using yet.

"Why have you polluted my hell with Baphomet's trash?" the Reaper's cold voice nearly froze Malice to the core.

"Because if I killed her, she'd probably just end up summoned to my Earth again and I'd be forced to do it all over again. My theory is that you can make sure that doesn't happen."

"Obliterating her pathetic mortal soul is a simple matter for me." The skeletal hand slowly rose.

This was it. She was going to be wiped from existence. All the plotting and scheming to live forever and this was what it amounted to.

"Actually," Conryu said. "I was thinking you could give her a job."

Had Malice's face still been capable of movement, her jaw would've dropped.

Conryu didn't seem to notice her reaction. "She knows all sorts of useful stuff about my world. Properly bound and compelled to obedience and loyalty, Malice could be a useful asset. Plus, isn't stealing a soul from Baphomet even more of an insult?"

The Reaper's laugh was like nails on a chalkboard to Malice's soul. "I picked well when I made you my Chosen. How would you like her bound? I'll handle the magic myself. That way she will never escape it."

"Thank you. I was thinking of something like what I did to Lucifer plus making it so she has to obey to the best of her ability any order I or Kelsie give her. With my orders overriding Kelsie's."

Malice finally got her mouth to work. "You expect me to follow orders from that useless excuse for a girl? I'd rather be destroyed."

"I think Kelsie would enjoy ordering you around for a change. Does that sound good?"

That last question was addressed to the Reaper, not her.

"Indeed. Now that I know how much misery this will bring her, I'm content that it's the perfect punishment."

The Reaper's will slammed into Malice and the world went black.

———

Conryu felt a moment of panic when the Reaper blasted away Malice's demonic form. Why he should care what happened to the horrid old woman was a question he'd never be able to answer. He relaxed as soon as he noticed the golden sphere that was her still-intact soul floating where her demonic form had been.

And a moment after that, Malice was back in all her dubious glory. She looked exactly as she had when he first saw her in the warehouse basement.

"It's done," the Reaper said. "You can summon her at your convenience. I've given this new body sufficient energy to maintain her for centuries while limiting its output. She currently has no more power than an ordinary human."

"That's perfect, thank you."

"It's a small-enough reward for all the good work you've done," the Reaper said.

Conryu offered a bow of respect. It was rare to catch Null in such a good mood and he didn't want to do anything to change that.

"I'll be heading back then. Malice, I'll see you shortly."

"I can hardly wait."

Her personality still left something to be desired, but fixing that was probably beyond the ability of even an omnipotent demon lord.

Conryu returned to the courtyard, collected Cerberus, and made the trip back to where they'd appeared. After a final goodbye pat, he opened a hell portal and stepped back into the real world. Since he'd been in Hell, everything looked exactly as he left it.

"Welcome back, Chosen," Kai said. "Did your meeting with the master go as you'd hoped?"

"Sure did. He was actually in a jovial mood, you know, for the Reaper. He seemed amused by my plans for Malice. She was considerably less amused, not that anyone cared. How are things here?"

"The security officers appear unharmed save for a few bumps and bruises. There has been no sign of further threats."

"Outstanding. Then other than the final clean-up, we're done here. I didn't see Tamaki when I got back."

"She's upstairs keeping watch."

"That was a good idea, though probably overkill. Let's get everyone out of here."

He walked over with Kai and she introduced him to Chief Gladyr.

"We're most grateful for the rescue," the chief said.

"Not a problem. Be sure to thank Kelsie, she's the one that called me."

"I'll do that, sir."

"It's Conryu. I'm not big on formality. Gather your men around and I'll get us out of here."

"I'll return to the borderland, Chosen."

"Grab Tamaki on your way."

She bowed and vanished.

As the officers were gathering the chief said, "She's pretty formal with you."

"Kai can't help herself, despite my best efforts to the contrary. I've made peace with it."

Conryu raised the staff over his head and they flew up and out of the basement. He kept on going straight up, blowing a hole in the roof as he rose.

"I'd ask you to be more careful," Artyom said. "But Kai explained Ms. Kincade's plans for the warehouse."

"That's convenient. I'll drop you beside your truck and wait for you to make yourselves scarce before I do it. That way you'll be able to honestly say you didn't see what happened."

"Smart. The insurance company might hire a wizard to investigate after all."

Conryu dropped them off at the armored truck and Artyom walked back with him towards the warehouse.

"I see now why Ms. Kincade puts so much faith in you. That was quite an entrance you made."

"Not my most dramatic ever, but it got the job done. I appreciate you helping Kelsie out with this investigation."

They reached his car and Artyom opened the door. "As chief of security it is my job. Maybe I'll see you around."

Conryu nodded. "Maybe."

The chief drove off and Conryu gave him five minutes to put some distance between himself and the warehouse. He used that time to create a wind barrier that would ensure that the surrounding neighborhood took no damage. Though if he was being honest, a good fire might improve the area. It would be damned hard on the residents though.

When the time was up, he leveled the staff and the crystal turned red. A fireball shot out and the explosion that followed sent a huge mushroom cloud into the sky. Looked like those chemicals were more dangerous than Kelsie let on. Happily the wind barrier not only kept the debris contained, it also muffled the explosion enough to keep all the local houses from having their windows shattered.

Satisfied with his work, Conryu opened a hell portal and stepped through. Kai, Tamaki, and Cerberus were waiting.

"Good work, you two," he said. "Tamaki, it was a pleasure to have you on the team. When there's more trouble, I'll be counting on you."

"I am at your disposal, Chosen."

"Never doubted it. Why don't you head back to the monastery and get some rest. It's been a hectic few days."

She bowed and quickly disappeared deeper into Hell.

"What now, Chosen?" Kai asked.

"Now we're going to see Kelsie and give her a present."

———

K elsie sat in her favorite leather chair, sipping a glass of wine. Soft music played and some of the tension had finally gone out of her shoulders. She'd heard from Chief Gladyr a few minutes ago, not a detailed report or anything, that would come later, but enough to know he and his team were safe. Naturally thanks to Conryu's timely intervention. It was a relief to know they were all okay.

She set her glass on the side table and stretched. So far, her best efforts to help Conryu had accomplished little more than to create more work for him. He hadn't even asked her for any favors, unless you counted dinner tonight and she didn't. Maybe Mother was right and she really wasn't cut out for this.

Someone knocked on the parlor door. She'd asked the servants not to disturb her, so something serious must have happened.

"What is it?"

"Mr. Koda is here, ma'am," a muffled voice said.

That was when Kelsie realized she was lounging around in her rather skimpy pajamas. She scrambled out of her chair, grabbed her robe, and slung it around her shoulders. "You can bring him here."

A little while later the door opened and Conryu strode through. He looked the same as always, jeans, black T-shirt, biker boots, and a friendly smile on his lips. As soon as she saw that smile she sighed and the last of her tension vanished.

"Hey, you good?"

She nodded. "Yeah, thanks for rescuing my people. I know it was a job you really didn't need."

"On the contrary, flushing out Miguel and Malice was tremendously helpful. The hellpriest escaped—the little shit has a talent for running away—but Malice has been dealt with permanently."

"How?" Kelsie wasn't sure she wanted to know the answer, but curiosity won out.

"I found her a new job." Conryu pointed at the floor and a moment later a black hell portal opened. Out of it rose the familiar figure of her grandmother. "She's on Team Reaper now, bound by the man himself. You seemed a little overwhelmed the last time we spoke, so I figured, who better to serve as your personal assistant?"

She stared from one to the other, trying to process what he'd just said. At last she asked, "Do you trust her?"

"Totally. Malice has been bound by the Reaper. She can't work against me, my friends, or my family. Even better, she has to obey any order I give to the best of her ability. She also has to obey you, as long as you don't try and countermand one of my orders. The first order I gave her was that she had to be nice to you."

"Grandmother hasn't been nice to me since the day I was born."

"And I'm sure she regrets it. Don't you, Malice?"

"I certainly do." Malice bit off each word like it tasted bitter. "I was a terrible grandmother and I'm sorry."

Kelsie nearly fainted. She'd never heard her grandmother apologize to anyone.

"So what do you think, could you use some help from the former CEO of Kincade Industries? Even better, since she's a demon now, you don't need to feed her or let her sleep. You can work her nonstop and she won't even complain."

Grandmother let out a very faint growl but didn't speak. Conryu's grin only grew wider and he seemed to be thoroughly enjoying himself.

"I suppose she does have a wealth of knowledge about the business," Kelsie said at last. "I'll keep her on for now. Could we talk alone for a minute?"

"Sure. As far as I know there aren't any world-threatening events that need my attention for the next few hours."

Given his lifestyle she figured he was only half joking. "Grandmother, you can go up to my office. Take the back stairs and make sure the servants don't see you. I wouldn't want anyone to faint."

"Yes, dear." Malice strode out of the parlor, her back straight and her stride firmer than it had been for as long as Kelsie had been alive.

When she'd gone Conryu asked, "Were you surprised?"

"Very. Grandmother doesn't seem too happy about her current situation."

"True, but her misery is just a bonus. I figured until you got completely settled in, having someone familiar with the business to help you would be useful. And for me, knowing Malice is under wraps and out of my way is a load off my mind. Don't worry though, if you get sick of her, I can send her back to Hell anytime."

Kelsie almost started crying. "You're not supposed to be worrying about me. The whole point of taking over the business was so I could help you."

"You're my friend, so I can't help worrying about you. And I'm sure having a rich businesswoman in my contact list will come in handy."

"Well you'd better remember to call me if you need anything."

"I will. Now I'm going to hit the road. I still need to stop in and see Maria."

"Say hi for me."

"Will do. Later." A door appeared in midair and he stepped through it.

The next thing Kelsie knew, she was alone. Assuming you didn't count her unnaturally friendly, demonic grandmother upstairs.

A hysterical giggle slipped out. Was her life improving or getting worse? Kelsie wasn't sure, but at least she was sure that she had one friend she could count on no matter what.

EPILOGUE

C onryu wiped sweat from his brow and turned a slow circle. He was standing on the sands of the Horned One's temple and it wasn't the unique architecture he was studying, but rather the ether. After destroying the temple core he'd returned to Crete to purify the temple. It was a tedious, but necessary, process. All the corruption had been burned away with light magic leaving the building nothing more than an interesting bit of history.

"I think we're good. What do you think, pal?"

"I sense no lingering corruption, Master. The humans outside will be pleased that you're finally finished."

He grimaced. The humans outside, as Prime called them, were a gaggle of archeologists eager to explore the most intact example of ancient architecture they had ever seen. The soldiers keeping the scientists back, Conryu felt certain, would be equally relieved to return home.

For his part, Conryu wanted little more than to never set foot on Crete again, nice weather be damned. Even a Mediterranean paradise got old when you kept finding corpses and fighting demons. Best make his report and get out of here.

"Do you want me to turn invisible, Master?"

"Your call, pal. If the startling doesn't bother you, it doesn't bother me."

"In that case I'll save my energy."

Conryu strode through the hole he'd blown in the side of the temple. Soldiers armed with automatic rifles stood at alert every ten feet. A hundred yards beyond them was the archeologists' camp. At least there was no sign of the scientists themselves which suited Conryu perfectly. A few of them reminded him too much of Professor Angus. Just thinking of the crazy old historian made him shudder.

"Excuse me," Conryu said. "Is your CO around?"

"Captain Kallou is meeting with the professors at the moment, sir," the nearest soldier said.

"That's fine. Let him know that the temple has been cleansed and the eggheads are free to enter. See you around." Conryu opened a hell portal and strode through before any questions could be asked.

"Congratulations on evading the bullet, Master."

Conryu grinned. That was pretty close for Prime. "Thanks. One more stop then Maria and I are taking a long weekend on a floating island."

He flew up on Cerberus's back and scratched behind the ears of his central head. "Take me to the monastery."

Cerberus barked and leapt into motion. Only moments later he stopped and barked a second time.

"That was quick. Back in a sec." With a final pat he opened a portal and stepped out into the monastery courtyard.

No ninjas were training which didn't come as a surprise. They were probably all still resting after helping him with the barrier spell.

The barracks door opened and Kanna emerged as always dressed in her black, form-fitting ninja outfit. She stopped a few feet from him and bowed. "Welcome, Chosen. How may we serve?"

"I don't need anything at the moment, but I did bring you a gift."

Her eyes widened slightly. "A gift, why?"

"Mostly for making you act as bait. I could tell it was hard for you." He dug into his pocket and pulled out a bone-white ring. "Here."

She hesitated a moment then took it from him. "This looks like the one you loaned me."

"In fact, it's identical. I had the forge masters make me a few spares just in case mine ever broke. It'll store the little bit of dark magic you shed. If, heaven forbid, you ever find yourself out of power with a desperate need to shift to Hell, it'll retain enough power to allow it. Think of it as backup. I wish I could give each of the girls one, but no one else has any excess power to absorb."

"I'm not worthy of such a gift. Certainly my petulant behavior doesn't warrant it."

"Please wear it anyway. I can't have anything happen to my grandmaster. If I need another homicidal lunatic seduced, who would I ask?"

She laughed and immediately slapped a hand across her mouth.

"That's bett—"

Horrible pain lancing through his arm cut Conryu off mid-word. It was coming from the Reaper's brand on his forearm.

Kai appeared beside him. "Chosen, what's wrong?"

"I don't know, but I need to get to Black City." He couldn't imagine what sort of horrible disaster had befallen the world that the Reaper felt the need to call him so aggressively, but had no doubt it would be bad.

A portal formed and he strode through. Instead of the familiar nothingness of the borderlands, that single step found him in the middle of the Reaper's throne room. Though Conryu couldn't see his face, it felt like the Reaper was glowering at him. At least the pain in his arm had stopped.

"Did I do something wrong?"

"You failed! A temple to Abaddon has been consecrated!"

Conryu stared, struck speechless by the news. How could this have happened without him noticing? Well, given how busy he'd been, it wasn't impossible. And that was the one guardian demon he'd completely lost track of.

Wait a minute. "How did you miss it?"

"There was nothing special to sense until the connection was complete. Now our enemies will be free to move as easily through Abaddon's hell as you are mine."

"Okay, that's a problem, but one I can deal with. One question. Assuming I kill the hellpriest and his allies then purify the temple, will that sever the connection and set Abaddon back to square one?"

"Indeed, but this will be the gravest challenge you've yet faced."

Conryu nodded. He didn't doubt that in the least.

AUTHOR NOTE

Hello and thanks very much for checking out Malice. I hope you enjoyed Conryu's most recent adventure.

As I'm sure you guessed from ending, more trouble lurks in the future for our hero.

If you'd like to support my work directly and be the first to get a copy of any of my new books, you can join my Ream Subscription. It's like Patreon only made by authors for authors. I post chapters from my current work-in-progress as they're written, so you can see how the story changes from rough draft to final edit.

Here's the link: https://reamstories.com/page/lhdcsvwjfy

Thanks again for reading,

James

ALSO BY JAMES E WISHER

The Aegis of Merlin:

The Impossible Wizard

The Awakening

The Chimera Jar

The Raven's Shadow

Escape From the Dragon Czar

Wrath of the Dragon Czar

The Four Nations Tournament

Death Incarnate

Atlantis Rising

Rise of the Demon Lords

The Pale Princess

Malice

Aegis of Merlin Omnibus Vol 1.

Aegis of Merlin Omnibus Vol 2.

The Complete Aegis of Merlin Omnibus

The Soul Bound Saga

An Unwelcome Journey

Darkness in Tiber

Depths of Betrayal

The Black Iron Empire

Overmage

The Divine Key Trilogy

Shadow Magic

For The Greater Good

The Divine Key Awakens

The Portal Wars Saga

The Hidden Tower

The Great Northern War

The Portal Thieves

The Master of Magic

The Chamber of Eternity

The Heart of Alchemy

The Sanguine Scroll

The Dragonspire Chronicles

The Black Egg

The Mysterious Coin

The Dragons' Graveyard

The Slave War

The Sunken Tower

The Dragon Empress

The Dragonspire Chronicles Omnibus Vol. 1

The Dragonspire Chronicles Omnibus Vol. 2

The Complete Dragonspire Chronicles Omnibus

Soul Force Saga

Disciples of the Horned One Trilogy:

Darkness Rising

Raging Sea and Trembling Earth

Harvest of Souls

Disciples of the Horned One Omnibus

Chains of the Fallen Arc:

Dreaming in the Dark

On Blackened Wings

Chains of the Fallen Omnibus

The Complete Soul Force Saga Omnibus

Other Fantasy Novels:

The Squire

Death and Honor Omnibus

The Rogue Star Series:

Children of Darkness

Children of the Void

Children of Junk

Rogue Star Omnibus Vol. 1

Children of the Black Ship

ABOUT THE AUTHOR

James E. Wisher is a writer of science fiction and fantasy novels. He's been writing since high school and reading everything he could get his hands on for as long as he can remember.

To learn more:
www.jamesewisher.com
james@jamesewisher.com